A special gift for readers of

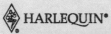

Two original novellas
written by a real-life mother and daughter,
just in time for Mother's Day.

Dear Reader,

Words can't express the honor and privilege it has been to work with my mother on this project we've called *A Mother's Wedding Day*.

As a child I grew up hearing the tapping of the typewriter as a new book was being written. My mom is my hero and my best friend. Since I can remember, I've loved reading, plotting and brainstorming ideas with her. Little did I know that the day would come when I'd be given the opportunity to have my first book come out simultaneously with one of hers. She's truly the most amazing mother in the world, one who has believed in me all my life, who has taught me that my dreams are only as big as my imagination.

This book has been nothing but a joy to write. Andrea and Sammi, the mother and daughter in our stories, have had great love for each other but there has also been pain and betrayal. It was a fascinating process to write how they find their way back to each other, and in the process meet and fall in love with the men of their dreams. I hope you love these books as much as we do.

Dominique Burton

P.S. The only thing I can add as Dom's mother is to say that it's been my joy to raise a wonderful, talented daughter I love to pieces. I used to tell her she had an editor's eye and never led me wrong. She has always lived her adventures. Now she's writing them and I marvel. We're both very grateful to our editors for making this special Mother's Day project possible.

ENJOY!

Rebecca Winters

A Mother's Wedding Day

Rebecca Winters
Dominique Burton

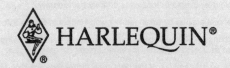

HARLEQUIN®

TORONTO • NEW YORK • LONDON
AMSTERDAM • PARIS • SYDNEY • HAMBURG
STOCKHOLM • ATHENS • TOKYO • MILAN • MADRID
PRAGUE • WARSAW • BUDAPEST • AUCKLAND

If you purchased this book without a cover you should be aware that this book is stolen property. It was reported as "unsold and destroyed" to the publisher, and neither the author nor the publisher has received any payment for this "stripped book."

Recycling programs
for this product may
not exist in your area.

ISBN-13: 978-0-373-75306-2

A MOTHER'S WEDDING DAY

Copyright © 2010 by Harlequin Books S.A.

The publisher acknowledges the copyright holder of the individual works as follows:

A MOTHER'S SECRET
Copyright © 2010 by Rebecca Winters.

A DAUGHTER'S DISCOVERY
Copyright © 2010 by Dominique Burton.

All rights reserved. Except for use in any review, the reproduction or utilization of this work in whole or in part in any form by any electronic, mechanical or other means, now known or hereafter invented, including xerography, photocopying and recording, or in any information storage or retrieval system, is forbidden without the written permission of the publisher, Harlequin Enterprises Limited, 225 Duncan Mill Road, Don Mills, Ontario M3B 3K9, Canada.

This is a work of fiction. Names, characters, places and incidents are either the product of the author's imagination or are used fictitiously, and any resemblance to actual persons, living or dead, business establishments, events or locales is entirely coincidental.

This edition published by arrangement with Harlequin Books S.A.

For questions and comments about the quality of this book, please contact us at Customer_eCare@Harlequin.ca.

® and TM are trademarks of the publisher. Trademarks indicated with ® are registered in the United States Patent and Trademark Office, the Canadian Trade Marks Office and in other countries.

www.eHarlequin.com

Printed in U.S.A.

CONTENTS

ABOUT THE AUTHORS

Rebecca Winters, whose family of four children has now swelled to include five beautiful grandchildren, lives in Salt Lake City, Utah, in the land of the Rocky Mountains. With canyons and high alpine meadows full of wildflowers, she never runs out of places to explore. They, plus her favorite vacation spots in Europe, often end up as backgrounds for her romance novels, because writing is her passion, along with her family and church. Rebecca loves to hear from readers. If you wish to e-mail her, please visit her Web site at www.cleanromances.com.

As a young girl, with a writer for a mom and three brothers, **Dominique Burton** lived in the imaginary world of books such as *Anne of Green Gables* and movies starring Indiana Jones. Much of the time she would write and act out her own stories with Harrison Ford as the hero. Not too shabby for a seven-year-old! Dominique loves Europe, and at twenty got the wild notion to buy an around-the-world, one-way plane ticket. For six months she circled the globe alone, studying Italian, learning about other cultures, scuba diving and having a blast. She graduated from the University of Utah with a bachelor's degree in history. She now lives in South Jordan, Utah, with her two amazing children. If she's not writing or reading she's out running. A few years ago Dominique had the privilege of running the Boston Marathon. To learn more, go to www.dominiqueburton.com.

A MOTHER'S SECRET

Rebecca Winters

A Mother's Wedding Day is dedicated to
my beloved mother who passed away a year ago
at ninety-five years of age. She always believed in
me. One night after she'd listened to some editors
on the Johnny Carson show, she phoned me
and said, "I found out you need an agent to
get your manuscript published.
Find one, darling, and send it in. It's wonderful!"

Thank heaven for mothers,
whoever and wherever you are.

Chapter One

The house was too quiet for Andrea Danbury's peace of mind. She walked over to the closed bedroom door and knocked. "Steve? Are you up yet?"

No response. She put his breakfast tray on the floor and tapped again before opening it. What she saw had become all too familiar. Steve de Roussillac, her employer of twenty-three years, lay across the bedclothes, so hungover from alcohol he wouldn't be up for hours.

There was no use trying to rouse him.

Three months ago his wife had divorced him. Since then his health had been going downhill and he barely touched the meals Andrea fixed for him. She was alarmed by his weight loss and knew he needed to see a doctor—maybe several. But only his son, Max, could influence him to get the medical help he needed. Unfortunately, it didn't look as if that miracle would come to pass.

Andrea found it tragic that since the divorce, Max had come to St. Helena only once. Though he was a mere hour and a half away, he might as well live on another planet for all his pining father saw of him. She was really frightened for Steve and knew something had to be done.

With nothing more to be accomplished right now, she

picked up the tray and left the main house for the cottage around back, where she lived and had her own art studio. She checked her watch. Ten after nine. Her mind made up, she reached for her cell phone and called 4-1-1 for the number of the Chandler Banking Corporation.

When Andrea was connected, she had to listen to a long menu before she could press 0 for a live voice. Eight rings represented an eternity. She almost lost courage.

"Chandler Corporation. How may I direct your call?"

"I'd like to speak to Max de Roussillac, but I don't know his extension."

"Just a moment please."

Thirty-eight-year-old Max Chandler de Roussillac was the newest and youngest CEO ever to rise to that position in the Chandler Banking Corporation of San Francisco. His mother, Helen Chandler, Steve's ex-wife, was one of *the* Chandlers of the Bay area, but Steve swore it was brains, not nepotism, that had put his son on top.

Andrea's heart raced in trepidation. Whether he was in his office or out of the country doing international banking business was anyone's guess. She broke out in a cold sweat just contemplating their imminent conversation. It meant trespassing on two people's lives.

She didn't have the legal right, but had to do something quick. Not only Steve's emotional and physical health, but the welfare of the vineyard itself were on a downward spiral with no hope of a reversal.

Steve might resent her for interfering, but she loved him too much as a friend to stand by and watch him waste away from grief over a failed marriage and its aftermath.

"Mr. de Roussillac's office."

Her hand tightened on the phone. "May I speak to him, please?"

"He's been in Zurich and is flying home today. I've been advised he'll be in early tomorrow. If you'll leave your name and number, I'll make certain he returns your call."

After a debate with herself Andrea said, "This is personal. I'll call him back."

"You're sure?"

"Yes. Thank you."

She hung up, determined that if he turned out to be too busy to take her call first thing in the morning, then she would drive to San Francisco and talk to him face-to-face.

Over the last two months Max had not so much as called his father. Every day Steve would wonder aloud how his son was doing. Whether he would come by soon. Max's cruelty to his father by his absence, let alone his silence, was anathema to Andrea, but she couldn't do anything about that right now.

Max's dark, lean looks made him an exceptionally attractive man. But it was what was on the inside that counted, and Andrea could not understand why the man had turned against his father. Grown cold like his mother.

Helen was known as one of the great beauties of the Bay area. When Steve had first introduced her to Andrea, she could see his wife's reputation was well deserved. Steve was good-looking himself. It explained why Max, who'd inherited the Chandler height, was such a striking man.

Over the years she'd watched him and his mother come and go from the main house. Helen had been friendly to her in the beginning, but over time her visits became more infrequent and she rarely did anything but nod to Andrea.

According to Steve, theirs was a tempestuous love affair. They came from different worlds. He was a son of the soil and didn't fit into the Chandlers' social world. Many differences, including his pride and her inflexibility, drove them apart. Then came the shock, three months ago, when Steve told Andrea his marriage was over.

What was most important to Andrea was rescuing her employer and friend from slowly killing himself.

In a half hour she had a ten-o'clock business appointment, and she needed to get going. Her prospective client wanted to see some of her hand-painted ceramic tile samples before redoing her kitchen.

Within minutes, Andrea was in her car and driving around the main house to where the road met the highway. She was on her way to Rutherford, the town where she'd been born forty-one years earlier, seven miles southeast of the de Roussillac vineyard in St. Helena. Other charming towns like Rutherford, Oakville and Calistoga dotted the fertile Napa Valley, an area north of San Francisco renowned for its wine making.

In her opinion the de Roussillac wine was extraordinary, but this last year the vineyard had been neglected because of Steve's depression. And further inattention and everything he'd worked for—the very reputation built over four generations of de Roussillac wine produced here—would be lost.

According to the foreman, Jim Harvey, the winery had been losing revenue for the last year. He'd been forced to let some of the crew go. Deep down, Andrea wished Steve would let Jim go, and hire another manager.

Jim was lazy. Steve should have found another vintner to replace him years ago, but Andrea didn't feel it appropriate for her to talk to her boss about that.

All this weighed on her mind while she went along with her day. Passing her favorite florist, she bought some freshly cut flowers to take to her aunt in the Bellflower Nursing Home in Rutherford before starting back.

Edna Green was actually her great-aunt on her mother's

side. Long ago, she had taken Andrea in after her parents had been killed in an horrific freeway accident. It was a huge task to raise a devastated fourteen-year-old girl. Despite her drinking problem, Edna had a heart of gold and had looked after her the best she could.

By age seventeen Andrea had graduated from high school and was working as a waitress at a restaurant in Rutherford. Chris Engstrom, a pilot who'd come down from Alaska to work, started eating there, and they fell in love. As soon as he made enough money, he'd planned to marry her.

When Andrea discovered she was pregnant, her aunt had let Chris move into the tiny apartment with her and her aunt and live with them until the baby was born and they could get a place of their own. Chris had insisted on paying the rent and buying groceries.

Tragically, he'd died before they could be married. His one-engine plane had crashed into the ocean and his body was never recovered. He didn't get to see their baby, Samantha, but Edna had been there for Andrea through her grief.

Andrea loved her aunt and owed Edna her life. Now things had turned around and she was able to take care of her financially and every other way. Though her aunt had suffered from Alzheimer's for the last two years and no longer spoke or knew anyone, Andrea visited her every day if possible. It was no sacrifice, not after everything Edna had done for her.

With a kiss to her forehead, Andrea left the nursing home to drive back to St. Helena. En route she heard her cell phone ring, but she was on the highway and her purse had fallen between the seat and the passenger door, where she couldn't reach it. If it was her daughter and she missed it…

She drove quickly around the main house to the cottage. Once she'd gathered her things, she rushed inside and pulled the phone from her purse. Sure enough, the second Andrea retrieved the message she heard Sammi's voice.

"Hi, Mom. I'm leaving you a voice mail because I can't bring myself to talk to you in person. Vietnam's heat is oppressive and the constant language barriers have gotten to me, but I've been contracted for this photo shoot so I'm just going to have to deal with it. I'll be here two weeks before I leave for Thailand. In an emergency you can always reach me by e-mail. Give Aunty Ed a hug from me. Say hi to Steve."

Too soon came the click. Andrea's heart plummeted. In despair, she sank down in one of the kitchen chairs and buried her face in her hands.

Her daughter had been so deeply wounded by what Andrea had done—or hadn't done, whatever way you chose to look at it—she'd left for the Far East and could no longer bring herself to have a direct conversation with her own mother. It haunted Andrea, who feared she might never be able to mend the terrible breach between them.

It was her fault for never telling Sammi the whole truth about her father. Though she knew he'd been killed in a plane he'd leased to fly advertising banners, Sammi wasn't aware he had extended family who might still be living in Alaska.

Four days ago, her daughter had accidentally found her father's journal while cleaning out a closet. It had been hiding in one of the many zippered compartments of his old backpack. Years earlier Andrea had put the pack in a carton filled with books and other items she couldn't bring herself to look at. She hadn't known the journal existed. There were brief references to family. A smattering of pictures.

In one of them he and another man, both grinning, were holding up a huge salmon they'd just caught. In another he had his arms around a pregnant Andrea, and wore a broad smile on his attractive face. One more showed him with his parents.

The unearthed evidence had shocked Andrea, but it had shattered Sammi.

"I have grandparents and you never told me?"

Desperate for her daughter to understand, Andrea had explained that though Chris had kept in touch with his parents, he hadn't told them about his personal life because he'd always felt he didn't measure up, and needed to prove something. She knew he sent some of his salary home, but he'd never explained to her why.

He'd said that when he became a success he would take Andrea and their child to Alaska to meet his family, but not before. His decision had hurt her deeply. She'd realized he hadn't told her everything about his life before he met her, and this slowly ate away at her newfound happiness.

Maybe he'd been nervous because she wasn't the kind of woman his parents would have wanted for their son. Or perhaps he'd been embarrassed to be a thirty-two-year-old man who'd gotten a seventeen-year-old pregnant. Andrea had looked older for her age. At the time they met, he'd assumed she was at least twenty, and she'd let him believe it until she'd been forced to tell him the truth.

In all likelihood he'd regretted getting involved with her. Whatever his reasons for not wanting his parents to know of her or the baby, she'd lost confidence in herself. Even before he was killed she'd been so vulnerable. She'd feared he'd fallen out of love with her.

At seventeen she'd understood so little about him. Their passion had been short-lived, and he'd died before she'd been given much-needed answers. By the time Sammi was old enough to hear the truth, Andrea didn't have the confidence to contact Chris's parents, who had no idea she existed.

With hindsight, Andrea realized she'd been too emotionally immature to deal with the situation in a forthright manner and get in touch with his parents anyway. Every decision made had been the wrong one, but she'd never dreamed that twenty-three years later her daughter would unearth a secret that had brought on this crisis. Because Andrea had remained silent, the omission had erected a wall between her and Sammi too high to scale.

The day before yesterday Sammi had left St. Helena. On her way out the door she'd turned to Andrea in anger. *"After I've finished my commitment in Thailand, I'm flying straight to Alaska to find my grandparents, if they're alive!"*

The memory of that painful moment caused Andrea to shudder. Her thoughts flew back to the months after Sammi had been born and Andrea had set out to find a job that would allow her to support both Sammi and her aunt, as well as spend time with her daughter. She'd discovered that Steve de Roussillac, the married owner of a vineyard in St. Helena, had been advertising for a woman to do occasional housekeeping and work in the wine-tasting room.

Tourists from all over came to sample the Napa Valley wines. The de Roussillac family produced Riesling, a wine that was slowly gaining popularity in the region. Her job came with free room and board plus a salary. Andrea felt it was heaven-sent because the cottage was a good deal bigger than the apartment. There was more room for the three of them.

With Andrea holding down a steady job, her aunt didn't have to worry about money. Andrea could keep her daughter with her while she worked. Best of all, Steve, who lived in the main house when he wasn't with his wife in San Francisco, was very kind. He appeared to be the dream boss.

In the end Andrea had done everything humanly possible

to make a good life for Sammi and Edna, and be the perfect employee. Over time Steve became more like a favorite grandfather to Sammi. To Andrea's mind he brought a certain stability to their world. The man whom she'd discovered was in a tumultuous marriage had turned out to be Andrea's best friend. He'd helped her through her darkest period.

Another wave of sadness swept through her. Steve was the one who needed help now, but she was meeting with little success in that department.

While she sat there in sorrow, it suddenly dawned on her she was due to open up the tasting room located in the front of the main house. She jumped up to wash her face and redo her makeup before heading over there. Work was supposed to be a panacea for suffering. Since Sammi had bolted, work was the only thing saving Andrea from wallowing in pain.

At the end of the day, she locked up and returned to the cottage. After she got ready for bed, she went into the small living room she'd converted into a studio with a kiln. For the next two hours she worked on some commissioned tiles, until she grew too drowsy to paint.

The next morning was a repeat of the day before. She found Steve in bed, unconscious. She started a load of wash and cleaned up his room, then hurried back to the cottage to follow through with her own agenda.

Promptly at nine she phoned the bank and was told Mr. de Roussillac was on the other line. At least he had returned!

"Do you want to leave your name and number and he'll call you back?"

"I'd rather hold," Andrea told his secretary.

"It could be a long wait."

"I'll risk it."

"Very well."

Andrea played the game with his secretary for fifteen minutes. She had to give the woman high marks for going along with her. As she was about to hang up, a deep male voice came on the line.

"Max de Roussillac speaking."

Chapter Two

Did she detect impatience in his voice? If so, it would fit with her low opinion of him. "Max? It's Andrea Danbury."

After a brief silence he said, "I never thought the day would come when you would seek me out." He kept his voice civil. "Were you the woman who called yesterday for personal reasons?"

"Yes."

"If you'd left a number, I would have phoned you back immediately. What can I do for you?"

"Nothing for me," Andrea answered quietly. "Your father's in a bad way. He's been drinking too much and needs you."

There was a sustained silence before Max said, "Do you mean he's in the hospital?"

His question pushed her anger over the top. "I take it he needs to be on his deathbed before you would show a modicum of concern? Let me tell you something. He's a greater man than you'll ever hope to be. As for answering your question, no, he's not in the hospital, but if he goes on languishing, he'll end up there."

"Languishing?"

"Yes. Since the divorce he hasn't been himself. Lately, he's taken a turn for the worse."

When she heard Max's sharp intake of breath, she knew she'd hit another nerve.

"He's ill. If I have to explain his state of mind to you, then you're not the brilliant man he constantly brags about who has taken the Chandler Corporation to unprecedented heights.

"Every morning I leave the cottage and walk over to the house to fix his breakfast, but he just toys with it. Or doesn't eat it at all. In case you didn't know, he has stopped answering the phone. The manager calls *me* at the cottage now, wanting instructions from your father.

"I'm not a vintner! I serve customers during wine-tasting hours, and those customers are getting few and far between. My time is devoted to my housekeeping and wine-tasting duties for your father. In my free time I paint.

"If Jim Harvey comes to me again for help, I'm going to give him your number and tell him to call *you* from here on out." On that fiery note she hung up on him, too angry to talk any longer.

While she stood there, trying to calm down, she realized she'd just made everything ten times worse. But there was no right way to deal with Steve's son. The first time they'd met, in the wine-tasting room, she'd found herself strongly attracted to the dark-haired college student, even though he was twenty-one to her twenty-four.

It had surprised her she could have feelings for another man so soon after Chris's death. The two men were opposites in background and nature. Where Max had inherited his father's Gallic coloring, Chris had been a blond and was fifteen years older than Andrea.

In the beginning she'd attributed her interest in Max to the fact that he was Steve's son and had inherited many of his father's appealing male qualities. When he'd asked her to go out with him, part of her had wanted to say yes, but another part told her it wouldn't be wise to get involved with the boss's son. Rather than turn him down flat, she'd explained that it was too soon for her to consider dating again.

Throughout the rest of his college and graduate school years, he came to the vineyard to help his father whenever he got a break. Inevitably, he spent part of his time with her. He had a charming way with Sammi and her aunt. Just when Andrea had reached the point where she would have said yes if he'd asked her to dinner or some such thing, he no longer tried.

She didn't know if it was pride that held him back, because she'd turned him down so many times, or the fact that he really wasn't interested anymore. If that was the case, then she didn't have the temerity to make the next move.

Whatever the reason, by keeping him at a distance too long she'd lost her opportunity. It had turned out to be another wrong decision on her part. Now the time had passed to explore what might have been between them.

She filled her time with raising her daughter and taking care of her aunt, while she did her work for Steve. As the years went by Andrea's art career started to take off, and Max split his time between San Francisco and Switzerland, working his way up in the banking world.

Over that period of time Steve's marriage grew rockier. Helen hardly ever came to the vineyard anymore. Andrea saw less of Max, whose appeal had ruined her for the other men she occasionally dated.

It hit her hard when one day he'd unexpectedly appeared with a woman, a beautiful brunette like his mother. He'd brought Catherine Townsend to meet his father. Max had escorted her into the wine-tasting room to introduce her to Andrea. She was flashing a diamond ring, which could only mean one thing.

Andrea had had to fight her feelings to remain friendly, without letting him know how the news of his engagement had affected her.

For the next two months she went through what could only be described as Max withdrawal until Steve told her his son had called off the wedding. Andrea shouldn't have been happy about it, but in her heart of hearts she was. Then she received another blow: Max had gone off to Switzerland again, this time for six months.

After that everything seemed to fall apart. Helen divorced Steve, and then her father, the senior Chandler who was head of the bank, passed away. His funeral brought Max home to take up duties as the new chairman of the board.

Andrea saw him only once, when he came to the cottage looking for his father. She'd been in the middle of painting some tiles and told him to come in. After she commiserated with him about his grandfather, he'd muttered something indistinct. They'd stared at each other until she could feel the tension between them. Then she'd explained that his father wasn't at the vineyard and she had no idea when he'd be back.

To her dismay, Max left without saying anything. That was the last time she'd seen him. Andrea didn't know why he stayed away from his father. No doubt it had a lot to do with his parents' divorce. It killed her, because Steve was all heart and warmth. His kindness to Sammi and her aunt had made such a difference in her life.

If Max ever thawed enough to spend time with his father again, he would be impressed by the man who'd thought so highly of his son.

Over the phone she'd been tempted to tell him he was the luckiest man alive to have a father at all. Sammi wasn't as lucky. Chris had been snatched away before she'd known him. Didn't Max know how blessed he was?

Andrea wanted to blame it all on Helen, but she couldn't. The woman might have a lot to answer for in brainwashing her son against Steve, *if* that's what she'd done. Maybe she hadn't. Maybe Max had turned against his father for his own reasons, but he'd been a grown man for a long time now. It was imperative he take responsibility for their estrangement and do something about it.

Of course, Andrea couldn't say any of those things to him, because she was guilty of a crime so much worse. She'd prevented Sammi from getting to know Chris's family!

When Sammi had lashed out in her darkest hour, she'd accused Andrea of being evil for keeping the truth from her. *Evil* was a strong word, one she'd never expected to hear come from her daughter's mouth, but the word fit the crime. Andrea had the strongest premonition she would pay for that sin to the grave.

STILL REELING FROM THE unexpected phone call, Max stood at his office window overlooking the Bay.

For Andrea Danbury to phone him out of the blue about his father, he had to treat her call seriously. Before now she'd never taken the initiative to phone him for any reason.

At the moment Max was in the middle of delicate negotiations to merge a new banking group with Chandler's, but he couldn't ignore the reason for Andrea's phone call. Beneath her anger at him, he'd sensed her anxiety. His had been building, too. He loved his father. She'd said he'd been drinking too much. That didn't sound like the man he'd adored from childhood.

He buzzed his secretary. "Mrs. Reese? Would you reschedule my overseas conference call for some time next week? Tell the parties I'll get back to them as soon as I can. An emergency has come up I have to deal with. I'm leaving the office now and will let you know my plans later."

"Yes, sir."

Needing to change out of his suit, Max raced to his South Beach penthouse overlooking Rincon Hill. In case he found his father in even worse shape than Andrea had made out, he decided to pack a bag, so he'd be able to stay over. After writing a note to his housekeeper, who'd be coming in tomorrow, he left for the hour and a half drive through wine country.

He had to concede that the route along the St. Helena Highway was one of the most beautiful in the world. During the times he'd lived in and traveled around Europe, drinking in the culture and wishing Andrea were with him, he'd visited many of the wine-making regions, including those along the Rhine. Each had its own unique charm. So did the Napa Valley, where the first de Roussillac had settled and bought thirty acres.

Today his father grew the same kind of Riesling grapes growing on his great-aunt's *terroir* in Alsace, producing a dry, elegant white wine that was a rarity in the Napa Valley. But according to Andrea, the vineyard was going downhill. Max had been so caught up in banking affairs this last year, he hadn't taken the time to help his father the way he should have.

The news about him wasn't good. A guilty conscience could cause a man to drink himself into a stupor. If his father *had* been having an affair with Andrea, as his mother had claimed, then he ought to be feeling guilty for not having divorced Helen long before she'd divorced him.

Max hadn't known of his mother's suspicions. Without telling him, she'd filed for the divorce while he'd been in

Europe. It wasn't until he came home for his grandfather's funeral that she told him the reason she'd ended the marriage, which had been on and off and on again for years.

He didn't believe it at first—his father had always been an honorable man. To be married to one woman while he kept another on the side wasn't his style. No matter what kind of a marriage they had, his father had been crazy about his mother.

As for Andrea, she was an enigma to him. In the beginning Max had felt an immediate chemistry between them, but he'd suspected her grief over losing her husband had prevented her from going out with him at the time. After five years of her turning him down, however, he had to wonder if it was because he was younger than she was and she refused to take him seriously.

Her rejection had stung for a long time. By his thirties he was well into his career, and enjoyed relationships with other women.

Unfortunately, each time he visited his father, he found himself more attracted to Andrea than ever. It maddened him that she seemed so satisfied with her life. She didn't appear to require a man to make her happy, though when she looked at him, he could swear there was still chemistry between them. Maybe more so than before. That was what baffled him.

He'd felt it particularly when he'd introduced her to Catherine, but at that point he was an engaged man who had no business thinking about anyone but his fiancée. Though he'd tried, he couldn't make his new relationship work. Andrea always hovered in the shadows, coming between him and his ultimate happiness.

To his dismay she'd gotten under his skin early and had stayed there, even though he'd tried hard to forget her. Not even the beautiful Catherine had been able to erase her from his consciousness. Unwilling to go into a marriage when he wasn't a hundred percent in love, he'd been forced to break it off with her, causing her pain he hadn't meant to inflict.

As for Andrea and his father, he didn't sense anything going on between them except deep friendship and respect.

When Max had told his mother she was wrong about the two of them, she said she had proof from an eyewitness. Furthermore, when she'd confronted his father, he'd refused to answer her one way or the other and had simply granted her the divorce.

Since Max had never known his father to be evasive or intentionally cruel, he'd driven up to St. Helena the day after his grandfather's funeral in order to get the truth out of him. That had been two months ago. When he couldn't find him in the main house or the winery shed, he'd knocked on Andrea's door and she'd told him to come in.

He distinctly remembered it had been a rainy March morning, but you wouldn't have known it to see her padding around inside the cottage with a flouncy cotton skirt and simple white blouse covering her rich curves.

She'd been barefooted, her long, ash-blond hair flowing over her shoulders. The ultimate earth mother, with green eyes the color of nature. After being away so long, he'd hoped she would have aged—anything—so she would no longer live up to the images in his mind.

If anything, she was more beautiful. Every forty-one-year-old woman with a grown daughter should look so good. Max hadn't seen Samantha in ages. Through his father he'd learned she'd graduated from Brooks and was quite the photographer now. It came as no surprise that she'd inherited her mother's fabulous talent.

Andrea's studio was full of her latest landscapes. It smelled of paint and her own subtle, flowery fragrance. His natural instinct was to study each canvas and discuss it with her. She saw things in nature that intrigued him.

In the background he'd heard an aria from *La Bohème* playing. When he discovered Andrea was alone, working on a painting, he found he didn't want to leave. While she added another dab of color, she told him his father had left the vineyard, but she didn't know where he'd gone. That wasn't good news.

Before telling her he had to get back to San Francisco, Max asked about her aunt in the nursing home in Rutherford. They chatted for a few minutes longer about her condition. It wasn't until Andrea started to clean her brush that she looked up at him.

"Steve will be so upset when he finds out you came to visit and he wasn't here. Promise you'll come again soon."

Her entreaty reached inside him. Was she asking him to come to the vineyard for her sake, too? It sounded like it. He'd wanted to believe it, but in all probability it was more wishful thinking on his part.

Max had banged his head on that door too many times to bloody himself yet again. In the end he'd left the cottage, congratulating himself for not giving in to the impulse to do what he really wanted, and take her in his arms.

As he drove away, he'd decided he couldn't honestly see her and his father as lovers. Maybe he was reading her wrong, but he didn't think so. Nothing about his mother's assertions added up. Her eyewitness had to have been wrong.

He should have asked Andrea point-blank, but how could he? His father was the one with the answers. They would have to come from him. It was too bad that at the time of his grandfather's death, there'd been problems at the bank. Max had had to leave for Switzerland to straighten them out.

He had ended up being in Zurich for the last two months. He'd felt it best to put off the conversation with his father until he got back. This weekend, in fact, he'd planned to drive up to St. Helena and spend time with him, but Andrea's phone call had reached him first.

A few miles later he came in sight of the vineyard. When he'd been here two months ago, his mind had been elsewhere. Now he could see that a portion of it had been left unattended. As he drove in, he noticed things looked run-down.

The gray-and-white, two-story Victorian house with its wine-tasting room needed fresh paint. So did the bungalow-style cottage. Shrubs needed to be trimmed and shaped. The estate no longer had the polished appearance that had once welcomed the public.

He parked his car at the back of the house and looked around. *Shabby* was the word that came to mind, one he would never have associated with his father. Not in his work ethic, or his habits.

The divorce had done its damage, but guilt consumed Max that his father's decline, not to mention the estate's deterioration, had come about partly because of his own selfishness and preoccupation with other matters. Andrea had spoken the truth. He should have realized sooner what was happening and taken steps to help prevent it.

Little did Andrea know that part of the reason he'd stayed away this last year was because of his growing attraction to her, an attraction that should have died years ago.

"Max?"

She must have heard him drive in. He jerked his head

around to spot her running out of the cottage toward him. It brought on an adrenalin rush—his reaction every time he saw her. The blood hammered in his ears.

She was dressed in modest white shorts and a blue-on-white print blouse her figure did wonders for. In the last two months she'd had her hair cut shorter, making her five-foot-seven body look taller. The cascade of ash-blond silk swirled around her jaw as she ran toward him.

"Thank heaven you came!" she cried without preamble. Close up, her green eyes looked anguished. "I thought you were the ambulance from the hospital in St. Helena. While I was painting, Steve staggered over to the cottage to talk to me, and passed out."

With that revelation Max hurried past her into the house. His normally fastidious father lay dead drunk on the studio couch, in a pair of sweats and a T-shirt. He was unshaved, unkempt.

Max cringed at the sight. He felt for a pulse. "How long has he been like this?" No wonder she'd raged at him.

"When I found him in bed this morning, passed out, I phoned you. It wasn't long after that when he came over here and collapsed. I called 9-1-1, but asked them not to use the siren. He would hate to have attention drawn to himself. His pride couldn't take it."

Andrea understood his father very well, and why not? She'd worked for him for twenty-three years. By now they would have a fine-tuned knowledge of each other. Without looking at her, Max said, "You were right to call. He's ill and needs a lot of help."

"It will mean the world to him to know you came."

The tremor in her voice increased his concern over his father's condition. "Right now I'm afraid he's oblivious."

"But when he wakes up, yours will be the face he sees.

I'm so glad you're here!" she said again, with enough emotion for him to realize she was truly frightened.

"Thank God you were here for him, Andrea."

"I should have called you weeks ago," she declared.

"*I'm* the one who should have come months ago," he muttered in self-deprecation.

They both heard voices at the door; the ambulance had come. She hurried to the entrance. "While you deal with the paramedics, I'll go over to the house. Steve will need some things at the hospital. I'll meet you there."

Chapter Three

Of necessity, Andrea had to inform Jim that Steve wouldn't be at the estate for several days. She didn't give a reason why. If there was an emergency, he was to call Max. She left the message including Max's phone number at the bank on Jim's voice mail.

Andrea didn't want him knowing personal details about Steve. The vintner would probably slack off on the job even more, knowing the boss was away. The less Jim knew, the better.

With that accomplished Andrea packed an overnight bag for Steve, including his personal items and his wallet. After turning off lights, she locked the back door, then hurried to the cottage to change into a denim wraparound skirt and sandals.

Grabbing her cell phone, she locked the front door and left for the hospital. When she reached the E.R., she learned to her surprise that Steve had been transported to an alcohol treatment center outside Rutherford. The triage nurse gave her the address and told her Mr. de Roussillac's son would be expecting her.

The facility was only seven miles away, not that far from her aunt's nursing home. When Andrea approached the receptionist at the center, she was told to go through the double doors on her right and she would find Mr. de Roussillac in room E45. Andrea thanked the woman and headed there.

After knocking on the door and opening it, she was confronted by Max, whose solemn black eyes settled on her. Andrea was taller than average, yet she still had to look up into his face.

His silky, charcoal-tone sport shirt covered a well-defined chest. Her gaze dropped lower and she noticed how the gray trousers molded to his powerful thighs. When she could gather her wits, she realized the large, comfortable, no doubt expensive room contained an empty bed.

"W-where's Steve?" she stammered.

"Being examined and tested for blood-alcohol levels. I met the psychiatrist on staff a few minutes ago. He'll be here shortly to talk to us. Come in and we'll wait together."

He took the overnight bag from her hand. Their fingers brushed in the process, sending rivulets of sensation up her arm. She stayed in the doorway. "I just wanted Steve to have his things. I don't need to be here."

Max's dark eyes grew hooded. "Actually, you do. The doctor wants to talk to the person who's been around him the most and knows him the best. There's only one person who fits the description and that's you."

She swallowed hard. "I'm not family."

He cocked his dark head. "True, but you've been a trusted employee living on the premises for many years. That counts for a lot."

His logic defeated her.

"Hello," said a male voice directly behind her. Andrea turned to see a fiftyish hulk of a man wearing a lab coat. "I'm Dr. Shand." He shook her hand.

"I'm Andrea Danbury. When Steve passed out this morning, I'm the one who called for an ambulance."

"It's a good thing you did. Let's step inside and talk, shall we?"

Andrea had no choice but to enter the room. She found a chair at the round table over in the corner and sat down. Max, lean and fit, stood by the other chair, while the doctor sat on the edge of the bed with his hands braced on either side of him.

"I'm hoping you can answer a few questions Max couldn't. How long has Mr. de Roussillac been drinking this heavily?"

She cleared her throat. "I've worked for him close to twenty-three years. About five months ago I noticed he started having a drink in the morning. He would drink steadily throughout the afternoon. Then, little by little, I saw he was having another drink before bed. When I cautioned him, because I was worried, he snapped at me, which was totally unlike him.

"My aunt was an alcoholic for many years so I recognize the signs. The thing is, Steve has always been a temperate man. I hoped it was simply a phase he was going through because he was so unhappy. Unfortunately, he never came out of it."

The doctor leaned forward. "Do you have any idea what brought on the downturn in his behavior?"

Andrea could feel Max's eyes on her. "Yes. It happened the day his divorce became final, three months ago. Not long after that his ex-wife's father passed away. She phoned Steve at the vineyard. Whatever was said during their conversation seemed to turn him inside out. He went to San Francisco for the funeral. I don't know what happened between the two of them, but when he came back, he was a different man."

"In what way?"

Out of the corner of her eye she saw Max's body stiffen. "He closed up on me. I tried to get him to talk, but he withdrew from everyone, his foreman and crew. When my daughter, Sammi, came home between photography jobs, she worried because he didn't seek her out. She was the one who had to find him. That was very unusual for Steve, because he'd always treated her like a granddaughter."

Andrea noticed Max rubbing the back of his neck, a subtle sign that he was growing more disturbed by what he was hearing.

"Little by little he stopped socializing with the local vintners. He disappeared for a couple of days. When he came back, he told me he'd decided not to take his yearly trip to Alsace to see his cousins. When they said they'd come to California, he told them not to."

Max looked haunted. "I had no idea."

Andrea bit her lip. "I should have said something sooner." She turned to the doctor. "Steve's a kind, loving, generous man, but he just kept retreating inside himself.

"Perhaps the most noticeable thing was that he didn't talk about Max anymore. He idolizes his son." Once again her glance strayed to Max, who appeared stricken by her revelations. "I knew then he was reaching rock bottom."

Dr. Shand nodded. "You've given me enough information to proceed. In general, most alcoholics suffer from a problem of depression or bipolar disorder. Mr. de Roussillac displays the four classic symptoms. He drinks heavily despite being warned of the danger, he drinks alone, he drinks at odd hours of the day—like this morning, for instance—and his drinking has resulted in poor work performance. Max told me the vineyard and grounds have suffered over the last year."

She lowered her head. "Yes." What else could she say? If Max hadn't gotten the message by now that his absences made him partly responsible for Steve's troubled state of mind, then heaven help them both.

"I'd like to keep him here for several weeks or even a month, depending on his progress. After that we'll see about letting him go home at night."

Andrea got to her feet. "I've felt he's needed this kind of care for a long time, Doctor. I'm glad he's here and that you had a spot for him. I need to get back to work, but first let me thank you." She shook his hand again. "When Steve's better, I know he'll be thankful, too."

"Andrea?" Max called as she started to leave.

She paused at the door. "Yes?"

A grimace had broken out on his handsome features. "Don't worry about anything. I'll be staying at the main house for a while."

"That will thrill your father." *She* was thrilled by the news. Glancing away, she said, "I'll see you later." On that note, she exited the building, practically running to her car.

Right now she'd give anything to call Sammi and talk to her about this, but her daughter's anger made that impossible. By the time Andrea reached the cottage, she was too full of adrenaline to paint. Normally her craft grounded her, but that wasn't possible today. With her emotions exploding all over the place, she walked to the main house and decided to give the kitchen and the upstairs a good housecleaning.

Both Max's and Steve's bedrooms needed beds changed with clean sheets. Bathrooms needed scouring. The works! Though the winery had become run-down, she didn't want Max to find fault with her abilities as a housekeeper, especially now that he was staying on for a few days.

At four-thirty, she finished her work, then went to the wine tasting room and opened up for the few visitors who would come. While she waited, she phoned her friend Nancy Owens and asked if she'd like to meet for dinner and a movie. To her relief she was free. Her husband would be working late.

Nancy's college-age son was doing a poly sci spring internship in Washington, D.C. Like Andrea, she suffered from empty-nest syndrome. The two of them decided to make a night of it. They also made plans for the next evening. Following the Cinco de Mayo Golf Classic in Napa tomorrow, where her husband, Pete, was playing, the Owens were hosting a barbecue at their home in St. Helena.

After chatting for a few more minutes Andrea hung up the phone, grateful that for tonight she'd be with a friend. Otherwise she'd sit home agonizing over Sammi and waiting for the sound of Max's car. Knowing he was going to be around gave her a fluttery feeling in her chest.

Long ago she'd rejected Max because she hadn't wanted to make a mistake that would cause Steve to let her go. She'd needed the job security too badly. With her baby and her aunt depending on her, she hadn't dared make another wrong decision.

But you paid a price, pushing away the man you loved. She *was* in love with Max and had been for years. That was never going to change. She'd tried to care about a few of the men who'd dated her, but without the fire, it was no use.

Incredibly, the fire had always been there with Max. She'd felt its heat in the way his dark eyes flickered at the sight of her. Sometimes his deep voice grew husky while he was talking to her. When he walked into her studio, she was aware of his presence to the exclusion of everything else.

The knowledge that he would be staying at the vineyard for a while seemed to suck the oxygen right out of her lungs.

AT TEN AFTER ELEVEN Max heard a car drive around the back of the main house. He'd stayed at the hospital until his father had gone to sleep for the night. Since returning to the estate, he'd been listening for Andrea.

While waiting for her to show up, he'd started going through the accounts. Tonight his father had murmured something about them being in a mess, but he'd been so out of it the doctor indicated they wouldn't be able to have a truly coherent conversation until he'd detoxified.

Tomorrow Max intended to get the books up-to-date, but already he could see that over the last twelve months his father's profits had been dropping, enough to let some of the crew go. At this rate Jim wouldn't be able to receive the same size paycheck much longer.

Max waited until she got out of the car before he stepped off the back porch to approach her. "Andrea?"

A slight gasp escaped her lips as she turned in his direction. A hand went to her throat. "Max—"

"I'm sorry if I startled you. I thought you'd seen me."

"It's all right." She eyed him with that anxious expression she'd displayed earlier in the day. "How's Steve?"

"He's as comfortable as he can be for the time being."

"Thank goodness. You can't imagine the relief I feel knowing he's in a safe place, getting the help he needs." Her voice throbbed with the kind of emotion that couldn't be faked.

"My sentiments exactly." He moved closer. "Dad should have been getting medical attention much sooner, but that's my fault. I deserved everything you said to me on the phone and much more."

She shook her head, causing the ash-blond strands to gleam in the moonlight. "No, Max. I was much too outspoken. Forgive me."

"There's nothing to forgive. It's only natural you've been frightened, seeing him degenerate this way." On impulse he added, "I know you care for him a great deal."

"I love him," she said simply. Her eyes glistened with unshed tears. "When I lost my parents, at age fourteen, I wanted to die. My dad was kind and loving. After I started working for your father, I discovered those same wonderful traits in him. It was like I'd been led to him to help me get over my loss. Sammi thrived under his attention. I'll never be able to repay him for what he's done for me and my family."

Max's throat swelled. "Have you told him that?"

"Many times. That's why I feel guilty that I didn't call you sooner about his condition, but I knew you were so busy after being made head of the corporation. Steve has never wanted you to worry about him. He's always been so proud of you, you can't imagine."

Emotion gripped Max, making it impossible to talk.

"How do you feel about Dr. Shand? Do you trust him?"

Her earnest question deserved an honest answer. "These are early days, but I think he knows what he's doing," he replied.

"I want to think that, too. I'm impressed with his straightforward manner. Your father will like that."

"Agreed."

His dad had never talked to Max about Andrea, but he didn't have to. The fact that he'd kept her on at the vineyard for twenty-three years and never hired anyone else said it all. Theirs was as close to a father-daughter relationship as two people could get without it being related by blood. No wonder his father hadn't answered his mother's accusation.

The informant who'd poisoned her to the point she'd actually divorced his dad had been dead wrong. Before long, Max would prove it.

He slanted Andrea a covert glance. She looked stunning in a simple coffee-colored, form-fitted T-shirt and tan pants. If she'd been out with a man tonight, he would have had a heart attack at the sight of her.

Max had no doubt a long line of males showed up every time she opened the tasting room to the public. Did she continually reject them the way she'd done him?

It had been years since he'd asked her to go out with him. After the last time she'd shot him down, he'd sworn he would never give her another opportunity to gut him. But after their conversation just now, he needed answers to a question that had plagued him for too many years, and decided to risk her rejection one more time.

"I've been thinking about the partial loss of the vineyard and how we can turn things around. How would you like to walk through it with me while I assess things?"

Chapter Four

Prepared to hear Andrea tell him she was too tired and needed to go in, Max was taken by surprise when she said, "Give me a minute to freshen up and I'll join you."

He didn't dare flatter himself that she'd been waiting for such an opportunity. Most likely she wanted direction from him now that his father was in the treatment center. Still, the knowledge that she hadn't turned him down caused his pulse to speed up.

"Take all the time you need. I'm in no hurry."

True to her word, she emerged from the cottage a minute later minus her handbag. They started walking along the road that led to the entrance of the vineyard. "I know the winery business isn't my domain, but there is something I'd like to discuss with you anyway."

"I wish you would," he told her. "While I've been remiss, you've had to be the eyes and ears around here. Tell me anything that's on your mind. I promise you can trust me."

"I know that." She flashed him a quick smile that beguiled him. "You're Steve's son, after all."

Considering how much she revered his father, her praise was that much more meaningful. "If you're concerned about your position, don't be. Whatever is going to happen around here, you'll be needed now more than ever."

"That's good to hear." Her tremulous voice revealed hidden worries. "I wanted to talk to you about Jim."

Max had never cared for the man. The same age as his father, Jim had been working at the winery when Max's grandfather had died and Steve had taken over. There was something about the foreman's attitude that had always rubbed Max the wrong way, but his mild-mannered father had ignored it.

Max was curious to know what Andrea thought of him. "Go on."

"Since Steve hasn't been paying a lot of attention to things, I've noticed that Jim has been taking advantage."

"In what way?" Every few steps their arms brushed as they walked between the rows of vines, the full moon lighting their way. Sixty degrees was warm for this time of night in the vineyard. It was no use telling himself not to feel euphoric being alone with her like this.

"Instead of reporting here at eight on weekdays as he's supposed to do, he comes when he wants. Maybe you didn't notice, but neither he or his crew were here when the ambulance came for your father this morning."

"No, I must admit I wasn't aware of much." Max had been so shocked to find his father passed out, everything except Andrea herself had been a blur.

"A good foreman would have redoubled his efforts to keep the whole vineyard flourishing. He could have hired another man while your father was indisposed. Instead he let things go, and that's why this year's yield won't be nearly as much as usual. In my opinion he doesn't deserve the same salary, nor does his crew."

Max stopped walking to look at her. "You've been reading my mind."

A shaky breath escaped the lips he'd been dying to kiss for more years than he cared to remember.

"Sammi was really upset about it and begged me to talk to Steve. I know he kept Jim on because your grandfather hired him in the beginning, but Jim has let down his end and it isn't fair." Worry marred Andrea's lovely features. "What I should have done was phone you immediately."

The urge to hold her was too great, but the time wasn't right. Not yet. "The main thing is, you called me this morning and I'm here now. What else is on your mind?" In order to keep his hands busy, he put them in his back pockets.

"Since things have been getting run-down, we don't see nearly the number of tours coming to the wine-tasting room as before. I'm there for three different blocks of time between noon and evening, but often only one or two people come."

He frowned. "When do you get the biggest crowd?"

"At noon. If people came today while we were in Rutherford, then word is going to spread we're not a reliable establishment. That would kill Steve if he knew."

"For now we'll keep that to ourselves." Max took a deep breath. "Tell you what. Report for all three sessions, but if no one appears after a half hour, then lock up, so you don't waste your time."

"I don't mind, Max. It's my job."

"But *I* do." He took a deep breath. "Until things change around here, you should be able to spend your time painting rather than waiting for customers who don't show up."

The divorce had come as a painful shock to Max. But it had obviously been catastrophic for his father. The far-reaching consequences were only now beginning to surface, with a lot more to come, Max was sure.

"Are you all right?" Andrea whispered, eyeing him with concern.

"With your help, I will be." He gazed at her directly. "I won't forget your loyalty to Dad." Afraid if he stayed there any longer, he would do something that would shock her, he said, "We'd better get back. It's been a long day for both of us and I want to be at the treatment center first thing in the morning."

Her eyes held his a moment longer. "Please let me know when I can visit him?"

"I'll ask Dr. Shand."

ANDREA'S FITFUL SLEEP drove her from bed at six the next morning. She smoothed the hair out of eyes made puffy from crying.

Her tears had sprung from many sources. Besides her agony over Sammi and Steve, the walk with Max last night had opened her up to all kinds of feelings she had suppressed where he was concerned. When he'd been thanking her last night, her desire for him had been so great it was a miracle she hadn't thrown herself into his arms.

Coffee. Andrea needed coffee in order to get a handle on her emotions. She padded into the kitchen to fix it. With a little caffeine and sugar her mind might start to clear.

While she sipped the hot liquid, she closed her eyes in relief that Max was in sync with her over Jim. The foreman's poor performance had been unacceptable. Now that Steve's son was living on the premises and knew the truth, the head vintner wouldn't be able to get away with doing whatever he felt like.

After eating a piece of toast, she checked her e-mails. Her heart sank because there was nothing from Sammi. Andrea sent her a message anyway and signed it "Love you to pieces."

Once she'd responded to some clients' messages, she showered and washed her hair to get ready for the day. At ten to twelve, she locked the cottage door and stepped outside. It was lovely and warm and sunny. Perfect weather for a barbecue this evening.

There weren't any cars in the guest parking at the side of the main house. Max's black Mercedes was gone. He'd indicated he'd be leaving early for the treatment center to be with his father.

She walked around to the front portion that had been converted into a tasting room and restrooms for the public. As she climbed the porch steps, the sign at the side of the door mocked her. The de Roussillac Tasting Room Is Open Seven Days a Week, Twelve to One-thirty, Three to Four, Five to Six-thirty.

Being that it was a Wednesday, there probably wouldn't be a lot of customers. As she was opening up the place, her cell phone rang. Maybe it was Sammi calling in response to her e-mail. Andrea wanted it to be her daughter so badly, she clicked on without checking the caller ID.

"Hello?" she said, moving behind the bar.

"Hey, Andrea!"

It was Nancy. With everything else on her mind, she'd almost forgotten about tonight. "Hi! I was going to call you in a little while. What else can I bring besides hamburger buns?"

"How about a man?"

"Very funny."

"With the whole gang coming tonight I thought—"

"I know what you thought," she interrupted in a teasing tone. Andrea rarely showed up with a date. Long ago her friends had given up trying to matchmake. "Love you anyway. What time do you want me there?"

"Seven-thirtyish. Come early and swim. Have I got a lot to talk to you about. Mike called this morning and told us he's met this great intern from North Carolina. I heard him tell his father she's hot!" Nancy moaned. "He's supposed to be excited about working, not about girls."

Andrea chuckled. "Wait till next week and he'll probably be crazy over someone else."

"I hope you're right. He's too young."

Yup. Mike was only seventeen. Andrea knew all about getting involved too young. "I want to hear the details. Tell Pete good luck at the golf match. See you tonight." As she hung up, she saw the door open, and let out a quiet gasp to discover Max in the entry.

He strolled over to the bar, placing his hands on the counter. With a woman's instinct, she knew he could have married any female he wanted. If ever she allowed herself to think about the women he'd been with over the years, her envy—no, her jealousy—would drive her mad. It was better not to think about it, but right now she couldn't help it.

He was wearing an opened-necked, cream sport shirt, and jeans that clung to his hard-muscled legs. Andrea couldn't help but note some of his inherited French traits. Her gaze took in the slight dusting of black hair on his chest and arms. Like his father, he probably had to shave twice a day to avoid a shadow. These days Steve barely got around to it.

Max looked at home in this French setting of charming bistro tables and chairs placed on hardwood floors stained dark walnut. Among several framed Impressionist prints, some of Andrea's best oil paintings hung on the stucco walls beneath the beamed ceiling.

A smile quirked the corner of his mouth. "That mural behind you is priceless. Every time I walk in here, I marvel. The customers always go away talking about it."

Warmth filled her. "You're full of it, but thank you anyway." Years ago she'd painted a wall-size mural telling the de Roussillac wine story. It had been her gift to Steve for his generosity and kindness to her.

With the man's praise and encouragement of her artistic talent, she'd slowly developed a clientele for her oils. He'd insisted on displaying them in the tasting room. In time she ventured into painting ceramic tiles, and had calls for them, as well. Andrea owed Steve everything and could never repay him for his goodness, not in a lifetime.

Max ate a few of the olives and crackers she'd put out on the counter. "I came to get some more clothes for Dad. Before I go back to the treatment center I wondered if you could explain something for me."

"What is it?"

"I've been searching the books, but so far I've found nothing to indicate you've drawn a salary for the last four years. Why is that?"

"Four years ago I started making enough money from my artwork to stop accepting a salary from him, but I still continued to work for him. When he could see I wasn't cashing my paychecks, and demanded an explanation, I told him I could never make up to him for all he's done for me.

"He got upset and told me that wasn't acceptable. We argued. I told him I wouldn't take any more money from him, and planned to move out of the cottage with my aunt. Through a lot of hard study, Sammi had won a scholarship to get into Brooks, and was rarely home. Steve begged me not to go. I told him I wouldn't leave if he'd let me continue to be his housekeeper and keep running the tasting room. He accepted the terms and we've lived in harmony ever since."

While Max stood there looking stunned, a group of five tourists came into the room.

"Good afternoon," she called out. "It's a beautiful day, isn't it?"

"It is now," said one of the men, smiling broadly at her.

Max still hadn't moved. His dark gaze flicked to the man before centering on her once more. "I'll talk to you later." When he walked out, he left her bereft. No doubt he would be spending the rest of the day and evening with his father.

Six hours later she said goodbye to the last customer of the evening and locked up, before rushing back to the cottage to get ready for the barbecue. She decided to wear her white cotton dress with the capped sleeves. It cinched at the waist with a wide belt of woven rope she'd designed. Once she'd slipped on her white sling-back sandals, she hurried out to the car.

On the way to Rutherford she picked up the hamburger buns and a sweet roll at her favorite bakery, then made a quick visit to her aunt. Edna loved sweet rolls. After giving her the day's rundown, she kissed her cheek and promised to see her tomorrow.

A minute later Andrea arrived at the treatment center and took an extra breath when she spotted Max's car in the parking lot.

Chapter Five

"Dad? How are you feeling?"

"Strange." For the first time since Max had arrived, his father studied him as if he could really see him.

Max sat in a chair at the side of the bed, watching him. "Are you still nauseated?"

"Yes."

For him to admit it, it had to be bad. "Don't try to talk."

"I have to. Andrea was the one who called you to come, didn't she?"

Max sucked in his breath. "Who else?" The memory of it still played havoc with his guilt.

"She shouldn't have. You've got a bank to run. Why are you still here?"

Max had been waiting for his father to become coherent enough to carry on a conversation. Now that the moment had arrived, he had difficulty finding the right place to start. He sat forward. "I've decided to take the whole month of May off."

"You can't do that!"

"Being the CEO has its perks."

"You haven't told your mother about me, have you?"

The anxiety in his voice was a revelation to Max. So was

the switch in topic. "No. I called her this morning and told her I was spending some time with you."

"Promise me you won't tell her I'm in here."

That wouldn't be easy. "Let's not worry about that right now."

"Is Andrea all right?"

At the mention of her name, Max sprang to his feet. When he'd seen the way that tourist had been devouring her with his eyes, he'd wanted to tell everyone he was closing up the place so he could be alone with her.

"She's fine."

"I don't know how she does it."

Max stared down at his dad. "What do you mean?"

"Samantha has broken her mother's heart, but that doesn't stop Andrea from looking after me." *What had Samantha done?* "Is it true I passed out at the cottage?"

"Yes," Max murmured.

"I'm so ashamed."

"Don't be. You've been under a terrible strain."

"There's no excuse for it. Edna used to drink too much, but Andrea was patient with her, too. When the Alzheimer's started, she'd put her in the wheelchair and push her along the road so she could look out at the vineyard."

Tears squeezed out from beneath his father's closed eyelids. "Now, when Andrea needs me most, I've sunk to such a low level I haven't been there for her."

Max sat down again. "What do you mean?"

"Samantha's young. She doesn't understand what Andrea was up against at the time. When I think of what she went through and the sacrifices she made…" He grew visibly agitated and tried to sit up.

Filled with alarm, Max gently eased him back against

the pillow and pressed the call button. "Don't try to talk anymore right now."

More tears ran down his father's cheeks. "I've failed everyone—you, your mother…"

Aghast at what he was hearing, Max squeezed his hand. "You've failed no one." *It's the other way around.* "You need rest. Let the medication work. I'll see you tomorrow. I love you."

He kissed his dad's brow before heading for the door. On the way out, he met the nurse coming in. "Since my father woke up, he's grown more agitated."

She nodded. "I'll make him comfortable."

"Thank you."

Dr. Shand was right behind her. He stayed out in the hall to talk with Max. "I'd like your permission to try an experiment of sorts, but I need to talk to you about it before I broach it with your mother."

My mother? Dr. Shand was full of surprises. "Go on."

"Your father has rambled on freely about everyone but her. There's no question his depression stems from their failed marriage. I understand neither of them has had any counseling over the years."

"No. Not *my* parents."

"Then it's time to bring them together to talk."

Max let out a low whistle. His father didn't want her to hear he was in the treatment center. "I'm afraid they don't know how."

"Precisely. But his life has never been on the line before. If I make that clear to her when I ask her to come in for a first session, do I have your backing?"

First had to mean one of many. Naturally, there would have to be more if Dr. Shand hoped to make headway with either parent. "Of course."

"Good. I'm thinking next Saturday morning. By then your father will be well enough to deal with the elephant in the room, so to speak."

That wasn't very far off. Of necessity Andrea's name would come up. The mere mention of her would burn through his mother like corrosive acid. Max plowed his fingers through his hair. The doctor didn't realize what he was asking. "I don't know if she'll do it."

"I've a hunch she's been in a depressed state for years, too."

The doctor had just hit the nail on the head. "My parents have been a disaster for most of my life." *So have I.*

"Then you're with me on this?"

Meeting the man's gaze head-on he said, "Yes, but before you call her, there's something I need to do first. Then I'll phone you and give you the go-ahead."

Though the problem with Max's parents had started years before Andrea entered the picture, she was his mother's stumbling block at the moment. Until Helen was given definitive proof that Andrea and his father were friends, not lovers, then no psychotherapy would ever take place.

"Fine, but keep in mind time is of the essence where your father's recovery is concerned."

Max knew that, but there was so much more at stake here than the doctor could possibly imagine. His mother had flatly refused to tell him the name of her informant. After the funeral, when he'd come to talk to his father about it, Steve hadn't been at the vineyard. Right now he wasn't well enough for such a discussion. That meant Max needed Andrea to help him figure it out.

In order for that to happen, he would have to tell her his mother had initiated the divorce because of a rumor about her and his father. Knowing it would cause Andrea pain, he would have to proceed carefully.

"I'll get back to you as soon as I can."

"Good." The doctor clapped him on the shoulder before entering his father's room to finish his nightly rounds.

Max stood there deep in thought. As soon as he got back to the vineyard, he'd go over to the cottage. Andrea might not be there, but he'd take his chances. He'd been waiting years for a legitimate excuse to spend time with her.

Last night, he felt he'd achieved a slight breakthrough. Though the last thing he wanted to do was talk about his parents' problems with her, the situation had to be dealt with for everyone's sanity.

He strode down the hall toward the entrance, and was stunned to discover the subject of his thoughts coming through the main doors. They glanced at each other at the same moment.

"Max?" Andrea sounded out of breath and looked fantastic in a white dress that showed off her hourglass figure. "How's your father?"

"He's coming along. Dr. Shand's in with him now."

"I wanted to be here sooner, but we had a surprising number of customers this evening, and then I had to drop in on my aunt."

"Don't worry about it. The doctor said to give Steve a week, then you can visit him anytime you want."

"I'm glad you told me." She studied his features almost nervously. "Are you going home?"

"Are you?" he countered. "If so, maybe we could have dinner here in town first. I don't know about you, but I haven't eaten since breakfast."

"Actually, I'm on my way to a barbecue in St. Helena. My friend Nancy Owens and her husband, Pete, are giving it. Would you like to come?"

Maybe he was hallucinating, but those jewel-like green

eyes shimmering up at him looked sincere. "After waiting twenty plus years for an invitation, what do you think?"

A slow smile curved her mouth. "I wasn't very nice to you, was I?"

"No."

"I had my reasons."

"I'd like to hear them. Why don't I follow you home? Then I'll take you to the party in my car."

WHILE MAX TALKED TO THE men, Andrea helped Nancy carry the leftover food back to the kitchen. For the moment, the two of them were alone. "Thanks for a wonderful evening. The dinner was fabulous."

Her redheaded friend rolled her eyes at her. "It's not over yet. The Cinco de Mayo fireworks at the Lopez winery will be starting any minute." With the fire watch so high, it was the only show in town.

"We'll be able to see it on the drive back home."

"Why aren't you going to stay?"

"I'm afraid we can't."

Nancy flashed Andrea a knowing smile. "I wouldn't want to stay, either, not when I could be alone with a man like that. Where on earth have you been hiding him all these years?"

Nancy hadn't asked the right question. "He runs the Chandler Corporation, remember?"

"I'm not likely to forget. He's so gorgeous I thought all the women here would pass out when you walked in."

Andrea tried in vain to suppress her own feelings of excitement at being with him. "Max does his father's accounts and needs to finish them before he leaves for San Francisco first thing in the morning."

On the drive over to Nancy's, he'd told Andrea he would

be working on them while Steve was getting treatment. As for his heading back to the city, she'd made that up, but she didn't want her friend getting the wrong idea.

"There's a lot more than business going on," Nancy drawled with the persistence of a woman who'd been as much of a sister to her as a friend.

"Don't be silly."

"You've been lit up like a Christmas tree all night."

Andrea clapped her hands to her cheeks. "Has it been that obvious?"

"Only to me, but then I've had the benefit of knowing you for years. His presence provides the missing piece of a maddening puzzle."

"Andrea?" a deep, familiar voice called.

She swung around guiltily. "Max—I was just coming."

"There's no hurry." He moved closer.

It was too late to wish he hadn't said that in front of Nancy. "I'm ready." She turned to her friend and hugged her. "Thanks again."

Max shook her hand. "We both thank you. I was just telling Pete I haven't enjoyed a party so much in years."

"That's nice to hear. Now that we've met, don't be a stranger. Once it's June, we'll keep the pool open all summer. You and Andrea are welcome anytime."

His mouth, as well as his dark eyes, smiled. "I'll remember that." The man had so much male appeal, Andrea had to look away.

Together they went back outside. After saying goodnight to the crowd, they headed for Max's car and he helped her in. Nancy's home was only two miles from the de Roussillac vineyard. They drove in silence, but it was an easy one. As they pulled in, the first burst of fireworks lit up the sky.

Max flicked Andrea a glance. "Let's watch them from the veranda. But first I'd like us to program our cell-phone numbers. We need to be able to get hold of each other in an emergency or otherwise."

The otherwise part sent a shiver through her. After he'd helped her out of the car, she followed him around to the porch of the main house. They both perched on the railing for a better view.

One of the big starbursts seemed to trickle down like fairy dust and almost touch them. "Sammi should be here. She's always loved this holiday because it's like the Fourth of July."

Andrea felt his gaze on her. "Dad told me things aren't good between the two of you, but he didn't explain why," Max said. "Since I've never seen a mother and daughter as close as you, I can't imagine it."

"I wouldn't have imagined it, either." She jumped to her feet.

"Tell me about her. I've always had a fondness for her."

"When she was little, I was always afraid she drove you crazy."

"Anything but," he said with a contemplative smile.

Maybe it was the ache in her heart combined with the magic of the night. Andrea suddenly found herself telling him what happened the day Sammi found the diary and photographs in Chris's backpack.

When she'd finished explaining her reasons for not telling Sammi she had grandparents, Andrea was clutching the railing. "I did a horrible thing and deserve to have lost her love, Max."

"Not her love," he answered quietly. "With time she'll come to understand and forgive you, but she has to grow up first."

"She thinks she has."

"At her age, didn't we think we knew everything?" he reasoned.

Andrea lifted her head. "After my parents were killed, I'm afraid I didn't do any thinking to speak of. Over the next ten years I mostly acted and reacted to any given situation. It wasn't until your father gave me the opportunity to put my life together that I tried to start making responsible decisions."

She fastened her eyes on him. "Steve believed in me when I didn't believe in myself. Much as I wanted to go out with his dashing college-age son, I feared disappointing him. That was the one mistake I didn't dare make."

Max's lips twisted. "Dashing?"

"Yes. Very."

"So it wasn't because I was too young for you," he said with a certain amount of satisfaction.

"No. Your age had nothing to do with it. But that's what I wanted you to think, because I didn't want to hurt your feelings."

"Hurt doesn't come close to describing how I felt. Devastated would be more like it." Max got up from the railing.

"I'm sorry."

"Don't be. I'm a big boy now. What if I told you I've been dying to taste your mouth for over twenty years? I think it's long past time I was given the opportunity, don't you?"

Andrea didn't know anyone could move so fast. The only thing that registered was the crush of their bodies as he began kissing the very breath out of her. Obeying blind instinct, she melted into him and slid her arms around his neck. They'd finally crossed a line that had been holding her back for years.

His hunger engulfed her in a mindless passion. This was the man she loved, the man she'd needed and wanted for so many years. The only thing that mattered was to get closer to him.

His lips roved over her face and hair before returning repeatedly to her mouth. Their kisses deepened until Andrea was no longer aware of her surroundings. As if they had a will of their own, her hands slid inside his suit jacket to roam over his back, reveling in the play of hard muscles beneath his shirt.

He intoxicated her with his touch, molding her to his body, caressing her with wild abandon until her limbs felt disconnected. Her rapture was so complete, she was barely cognizant of a phone ringing somewhere. Maybe it was Sammi, but in her dazed state it finally came to her it was *his* phone.

"Don't you need to get it?" Andrea asked incoherently against his lips. "It might be the treatment center."

After kissing her long and deeply, he eased away with obvious reluctance, to check his caller ID. "It's Mom. I'll call her later."

He put the phone back in his pocket and started to reach for Andrea again. But she couldn't put the call out of her mind and placed her hands against his chest. "What if it's important?"

"After the years I've waited for this moment, nothing is more important than this," Max whispered against her mouth. Once again they were kissing with insatiable need. Andrea was on the verge of losing control when his phone rang again.

"You'd better answer it, Max. What if she's calling because it's an emergency?"

A resigned sigh escaped his throat before he allowed Andrea to escape from his arms. In the next breath he put his hands on his hips in a purely masculine gesture. "Since the divorce became final, every call from her constitutes an emergency in her mind. Which brings me to a grown-up problem I need to discuss with you. It has to do with my father."

Something in his tone created instant tension. "That sounds rather ominous."

"Only because I don't want to hurt you, but I know it will."

Chapter Six

The fireworks continued to light up the sky, but Max's words extinguished the joy Andrea had been feeling. "I see."

He rubbed the back of his neck absently. She sensed his hesitation. Though her trepidation was growing, she was intrigued, too.

"Did my father ever tell you why my mother divorced him?"

"No. I didn't know she'd even filed. One day he simply announced that his divorce was final." She spread her hands. "The news left me incredulous. For one thing, she's loved him forever. In their own way they've hung on to their marriage all these years. To suddenly divorce him made no sense to me.

"As for your poor father, I know how terribly in love he has always been with her. The shock was too much for him to bear. He simply closed up and started drinking more heavily than ever. You know the rest."

Andrea heard Max take a sharp breath. "Someone told my mother you and Dad were having an affair."

Andrea let out a sad little laugh. "Your father and I have put up with that gossip since the day he hired me. We always blew it off. So did your mother. In the beginning, tourists coming to the tasting room thought Sammi was our child. There've been times when Steve and I have hugged in happiness or in pain. Any number of people could have seen us do that."

His expression grew bleak. "This had to be as recently as five months ago when Mother decided to serve Dad with papers. The person in question said they were an eyewitness."

"To what? Intimacy?"

Max paced for a moment before halting in front of her. "Who would have seen you with him who might have misunderstood what they saw?"

"If you're talking in the main house, no one. I'm in his bedroom every day cleaning up, making the bed, washing his clothes. In the last few months I've served him breakfast in bed more often than not because he has been too hungover to get up. Several times I've helped him out of bed so he could make it to the shower. I've also brought in the mail and sat on a chair at the side of mattress to read it to him, when his headaches were too bad to focus."

"Did anyone ever see you at those times?"

"Only Sammi, when she was home for a day or two at a time before going off on another photo shoot."

"What about my mother?"

"I haven't seen her since before the divorce. Maybe she came in the house while I was working and didn't announce herself, but after twenty-three years I can't see her doing that."

"Nor can I." Max rubbed the side of his hard jaw. "In order for my mother to believe the lie, it had to come from someone she trusted implicitly."

"Your parents used to entertain a lot. It could be any number of their friends, maybe even one of your French relatives who came to California for visits. They all love her so much. Your poor mother. I wish she would have told Steve what she'd heard and who told her. He would have gotten to the bottom of it in an instant."

Max eyed her with compassion. "Tonight you told me you lost confidence during your marriage to Sammi's father. I don't think my mother is so different. Beneath all her polish, she's more vulnerable than most people know, and was too afraid to ask."

Feeling sick inside, Andrea moved to the porch steps. Looking back at him, she said, "Sammi once told me something Jim said about it not looking good for men clients to come in and out of the cottage. People might get the wrong idea.

"I was disgusted he'd said anything to Sammi, and re-minded her the studio was my place of business, so not to worry about it." She felt a pain too deep for tears. "I should have looked for another job and moved away a long time ago. But I was so comfortable with the life I'd made here, it never occurred to me I was hurting your mother."

Max shook his dark head. "We already know Dad wouldn't let you go. He could never have replaced you."

"Of course he could." Her voice throbbed. "After all these years, it never occurred to me your parents would end up divorced because of cruel gossip. Tomorrow I'll drive to San Francisco and talk to your mother. She needs to know the truth!"

As Andrea darted away, Max caught up to her and turned her around to face him. "I couldn't agree more, but don't do that yet. Dad doesn't want it to come out that he's at the treatment center. Not yet, anyway. There's something I have to do first. Do you trust me, Andrea?"

With their mouths almost touching, her breathing had grown ragged. "Of course I do."

"Then give me time to sort this out."

The pleading in his voice had her nodding. She slowly eased out of his grasp. "Good night."

THE NEXT DAY Andrea pulled up in front of the Casa Bonita at 10:00 a.m. and hurried inside. The restaurant didn't open until five in the evening, but this was a business meeting.

She'd worn her professional two-piece yellow linen suit for the occasion. Because of the exposure it would give her, this could be an important commission if she got it. Valerie Lind, the present owner, had told Andrea to walk on back to the manager's office. Since Andrea had worked here when she'd met Chris, she knew where to go.

"Oh, good, Andrea. Come on in and sit down."

Andrea took a seat in one of the chairs opposite Valerie's desk. An attractive, dark blond man, probably in his mid-forties, occupied the other chair. "Meet Brad Warshaw, who's in charge of the entire renovation. Brad? This is Andrea Danbury, the artist who painted the tile samples."

He shook her hand. His blue eyes lit up in male admiration. "It's a pleasure to meet someone so talented."

"Thank you. I've heard of Warshaw Interiors. From Napa?"

"Yes. Is that good or bad?"

She laughed. "Definitely good."

"That's nice to hear." His gaze lingered on her.

Valerie sat back in her swivel chair. "I feel fortunate to have both of you on the team, so to speak. As I told Andrea the last time we met, Brad, a friend of mine built a new home in Calistoga. When I went to see it, I was enchanted by the kitchen decorated with Andrea's hand-painted tiles. I got her name and called her to show me some samples.

"They were so unique, my mind was settled on what I wanted to do with this place. It has needed an overhaul for years, but I couldn't talk my father into doing it. This place is just one big, boring rectangle, with no real atmosphere for a Mexican restaurant.

"Now that he's passed, I'm free to go ahead with my plans. I told Brad I want him to design the place using your tiles as the inspiration, Andrea."

"That's a real compliment, Valerie." After the sleepless night she'd endured after Max had dropped his bombshell, she was pleased to get good news today. She'd needed something positive like this, especially when she hadn't seen Max this morning.

She ached for him. They should never have kissed. The events of last night had left a bittersweet memory, because she hadn't been able to get her mind off Helen's pain.

The man seated next to her eyed her speculatively. "I'd like to see all your samples. Would it be possible to do that today?"

His question jerked her back from her torturous thoughts to the present. "Yes. Could you come to my studio in St. Helena at three? If you don't see anything you like, I can sketch some ideas while we talk." She handed him her business card with its map.

He studied it for a moment. "Perfect. I'll see you then." He got up from the chair and shook Valerie's hand. "You'll be hearing from me before long."

"Wonderful. I can't wait to see what you come up with."

After he left, Andrea chatted with Valerie for a few minutes, then left for the nursing home to spend a half hour with her aunt. Her day flew by. Once she'd closed up the tasting room, she hurried back to the cottage to grab a sandwich before Mr. Warshaw pulled up in his Audi.

She let him into her studio. "Pardon the smell of paint. I don't notice it anymore, but my customers do."

"I like it."

"You're very kind."

His eyes told her he returned the compliment. "Valerie happened to tell me you're not married. Since I've been divorced almost ten years, I think she mentioned it for a reason. When the day comes that I might get you to go out with me, at least you'll know the most important fact about me."

"I'll keep that in mind." His approach was different, but she'd been in Max's arms last night and that was the only place she wanted to be from now on. With a smile she said, "The samples are over here."

In front of the wall with the fireplace she never used, she'd placed end-to-end banquet-size tables with stools. One held her tile samples and half a dozen portfolio-size folders with photographs of paintings she had for sale.

The other one she kept free to do sketches or whatever was needed. "Go ahead and browse. Can I get you a cold drink? Sprite? Pepsi?"

"A Pepsi would be great."

"I'll be right back." She walked through to the kitchen and got one for each of them. "Here you go."

"Thank you." While he drank, he moved back and forth. She could tell he was drawn to the Old Spain tile motifs. His hand hovered over one and he finally picked it up. "This tile you've called Alhambra is stunning and the design isn't too big. Every color is there."

"It's one of my favorites, but it's very delicate and would need a small room like a bathroom to bring it out. If we're talking a whole restaurant interior, I'd go to a deeper terracotta shade and a more intense green to balance the blue against the red and orange. It would be more dramatic. Let me put some pigment on paper so you can see the difference in colors."

She only took a minute to demonstrate. "What's your opinion?"

He studied it for a while before he smiled at her. "Never argue with the artist. Already I can visualize your tiles as a trim around the arches of the walls we'll erect. I'm thinking an indoor patio and loft area with a wrought—"

Andrea never heard the rest of his sentence because there was a knock at the front door, interrupting them. "Excuse me for a minute. It's probably another client." She put her half-full drink on the table and walked over to the entry.

When she opened it, her pulse started to race at the sight of Max standing there. "Hi." His gaze centered on her mouth. The memory of what they'd shared last night was still with her.

"Hi, Max."

"I can see you're with a client, but I wanted you to know I need to talk to you as soon as you're free."

This was probably about his mother. Andrea didn't have to think. "You're welcome to come in and wait. This appointment shouldn't take too long."

"Thank you."

Max stepped inside. He was taller than Brad, more powerfully built. She introduced them. After a nod to the designer, he picked up half a dozen of her painted fruit tiles. While he planted himself on the couch to look at them, she tried to focus on Brad, but it was almost impossible.

They discussed other tiles, but he kept coming back to the Alhambra. "Tell you what, Andrea. If I could take this tile with me, I'll return it after I've worked up a full color layout for Valerie."

"Keep it as long as you need to."

"I'm excited about working with you." He smiled, sending out vibes that he meant what he said. "We're going to transform Casa Bonita."

"I used to work there when I was a teenager. Valerie's right. It needs a lot of help." She packed the tile in a small carton and handed it to him.

"Thanks. I'll let myself out. When I've drafted some designs, we'll get together and go over them. I'll give you a call."

"Good. See you soon."

Chapter Seven

Alone at last...

Max rose to his full height and put the tiles back on the table. "You're a very gifted artist, Andrea."

"Thank you."

Their eyes met. She'd been aching to see him, but he didn't pull her into his arms. Andrea could tell he had other things on his mind. "I've just come from talking to Dr. Shand. He told me he intends to keep Dad at the treatment center for the rest of the month. In that time he's hoping for a breakthrough to help end his cycle of alcohol abuse."

"If that could happen, it'll save his life," she cried softly.

"That's the whole point, isn't it?" Lines darkened his arresting features. "But Papa's concerned about being gone from the vineyard so long. To alleviate any worry, I promised him I'd be here to take charge."

"Your promise had to have taken away his anxieties. Steve worships you," she whispered.

"Even if I'm the prodigal son?"

She heard a surprising note of self-criticism in his tone. "You're here now when he needs you most. That's what counts."

"We'll see," he murmured, sounding faraway. "First things first. Jim needs to be advised of the change in situation. A little while ago I saw him pull up to the shed. You were right—2:45 in the afternoon is a little late to show up for a job that starts at 8:00 a.m. Come with me and the three of us will have a summit meeting to discuss procedures from here on out."

Andrea blinked. "Procedures?"

"That's right. When you told your client that the Casa Bonita needed a lot of help, you could have been talking about the de Roussillac estate. This place needs a complete makeover. I want to get started on it this week."

His words charged her with exhilaration. "Give me a minute to change shoes." Her sandals slipped too much on the gravel drive.

"I'll meet you outside."

Andrea flew through the house to her bedroom and put on her sneakers. After running a brush through her hair and putting on a fresh coat of lipstick, she hurried out the front door. When she joined Max, he appeared deep in thought.

They walked the two blocks to the shed in silence. The private road ran alongside the vineyard. She could see his troubled gaze taking in the acres of vines that hadn't been pruned and tied last fall. It pained her to see so much of the grape crop lost for this year's harvest.

Farther on she spotted Jim's crew, working in the north end. Several cars and pickup trucks were parked outside the building. Neither Sammi nor Andrea ever went near the shed unless they were with Steve. Andrea disliked the stocky vintner, whose coarse language and wandering eye had repulsed her from the beginning. Of course, Max didn't know that.

Jim's office was at the front of the shed. Max opened the door and they walked into the empty reception room. "I think he's in the back. Wait for me."

She nodded, then rubbed her arms. The furniture needed refurbishing. Everything looked messy. Long before his drinking started, Steve had been in a depression. The problems in his marriage had taken their toll on him and the whole estate.

Andrea shuddered to realize how bad things had become. It seemed as if her whole life was about things she *should* have done. She should have waited to marry Chris before sleeping with him. She should have demanded he tell his parents they had a baby. She should have contacted Chris's parents after he died. She should have told Sammi she had grandpar—

"Andrea?" Until she heard Max call to her, she hadn't realized she'd buried her face in her hands. After dashing the tears off her cheeks, she turned around. "Jim will be right here. What's wrong?" He sounded alarmed.

She sniffed. "Ghosts. Do you ever have them?"

He took a fortifying breath. "You don't even want to know."

While his haunting admission resonated deep inside her, Jim walked in, wearing his usual T-shirt and overalls. He looked surprised to see her standing there.

Max nodded to him. "If you'll both be seated, we'll get this meeting started." The CEO from Chandler Banking was in charge.

Andrea took the chair next to the couch. Jim sat behind his desk.

"My father's enjoying a much-needed holiday. In his absence I've taken over the running of the estate and intend to make a lot of changes." She noticed Jim shift nervously in his chair. "But before anything is done, the emotional climate around here has to change, so we'll clear the air now."

Max was definitely working up to something.

"Jim? I want you to think back to a conversation you had with my mother five months ago. When she drove up from San Francisco and couldn't find my father, she came to the shed to ask you if you knew where he was.

"This was a very important day for her because she'd decided to tell my father she wanted to live on the vineyard with him for good. It was going to be a new start for both of them. According to her, you told her she only had to look as far as my father's bed or Ms. Danbury's, and she'd find him. You added that everyone who worked on the estate knew they'd been sleeping together for years."

Andrea moaned. Though she'd lived with the knowledge that there'd been gossip, the blood froze in her veins to realize it was Jim who'd done the damage.

"I don't know what you're talking about. I never said anything like that to her," the man muttered. "If she said I did, then it was her own jealousy talking."

"In other words, it's her word against yours," Max said flatly.

"Look—I've been working here twenty-five years without a single complaint."

"I'm wearing a mini recorder, Jim. It has been picking up our conversation," Max informed him. "If what you've just told us is the truth, then you won't have anything to worry about when it's turned over to the county prosecutor. If it's a lie, then you're going to be brought up on charges of slander and defamation of character of Andrea and my father."

Jim's cheeks went a dull red.

"I brought Andrea with me because she denies your accusations. Rather than a 'he said, she said' scenario, I thought it best for the two of you to confront each other so we finally get at the truth, before it winds up in court before a judge."

Silence filled the room.

"Name one time when you caught us together and found our behavior questionable," Andrea finally demanded in a quiet voice.

He shot out of his chair.

"Sit down, Jim. You're not going anywhere yet."

Max's command forced him to comply, but Andrea was on her feet now. "How could you have made up such a lie?"

Jim's head was bowed. Enraged, she moved over to the desk. "Look at me, damn you!"

He couldn't.

"For the love of heaven, what possessed you to be so cruel to a family that has retained you all these years? There's no one finer than Helen or more sweet and wonderful than Steve. He took me in after I'd just lost Sammi's father, and before that my parents.

"Chris was killed over the ocean. They never found his body! The Coast Guard told me he'd probably been eaten by sharks! I was out of my mind with grief and desperate for a job where I could keep my baby and my aunt with me. For months I suffered nightmares, imagining the hell Chris must have gone through. Sammi was all I had left of him. Steve helped me through that desolate time. He was like a father to me, and we got through our deepest sorrows together. The friendship we forged transcended anything your filthy, disgusting mind thought up.

"And how could you lie to Helen, when you knew she and Steve loved each other desperately? How dare you tamper with people's lives like that! A long time ago I sensed there was something wrong with you. So did Sammi."

Andrea clenched her hands into fists. "I don't know how you live with yourself. Steve was a dream employer, the best you'll ever see in your lifetime. How can you look your wife and children in the eye and not feel guilt that you've been responsible for the destruction of another family?"

Jim still didn't say anything.

"Your silence has convicted you, Jim. You're fired," Max declared in a chilling voice. "Gather up your things and leave the estate now. Your severance pay will be in the mail by the end of the week. If you so much as show your face around here again, you'll be arrested. Is that clear?"

Andrea headed for the door. "I'm going to be sick." She threw it open and started running down the road toward the cottage. Max didn't try to stop her.

A few minutes later she lost the breakfast she'd eaten earlier that morning. As she emerged from the bathroom on rubbery legs, she heard her phone ringing. *Please, God. Let it be Sammi.* Andrea had never needed her daughter so much in her life.

She pulled the cell from her purse and clicked on. "Hello?"

"Hi, Andrea. It's Judy. I'm calling to tell you your aunt woke up with pneumonia today. It's not severe, but she has a rattle. I knew you'd want to know."

"T-thank you, Judy. I'll be over as soon as I can."

After taking another shower, she changed into sage-colored pants with a white, short-sleeved top. Her most comfortable outfit. She would need it because she planned to stay with her aunt until she was out of danger. Andrea needed her own family right now, even if the older woman didn't know her own great-niece anymore.

As she drove away, Andrea could see Max in the vine-yard. He always stood out from everyone else. At the moment he was talking with workers in the north section. No doubt they'd already been told Jim had been fired.

With Max de Roussillac in charge, there were going to be many changes. She felt it in her bones. Most important of all, Steve had gotten his son back for good. Though her heart was breaking for the damage done, there was hope for Steve and Helen. As she drove toward Rutherford, Andrea marveled at the day's events. Max had uncovered the lie that would transform not only his parents' world, but his own.

So where does that leave you, Andrea?

Ah—that was a horse of a different color. Sammi still wanted nothing to do with her. The fear that they might stay estranged frightened Andrea, but she had to accept the fact that her daughter would never come home to live with her again.

It was time to leave the cottage. Today's showdown with Jim had marked a turning point. Nancy was a part-time Realtor. She'd help her find a new place. With the economy in a downswing, there ought to an apartment in Napa for rent at a good price.

Andrea also needed to find a studio with a workroom, probably at a downtown strip mall. She needed a gallery to show her paintings and tiles. The drive to see her aunt in Rutherford might take a little longer from Napa, but it was a larger city than the others in the area. Her business would benefit from the increase in traffic.

Most importantly, it would put her at a distance from Max. She'd loved him for too long. The pain had to end. What they'd done the other night was give in to their passion. It had been building for years, but now that they'd been able to work it out of their systems, this chapter of their lives could finally be over. For everyone's sake, it was better that she walk away.

MAX STOOD ON THE newly constructed deck off the renovated tasting room, where Andrea's mural formed the centerpiece. His gaze took in the profusion of newly planted flowers filling the beds. The brick pathways forming a geometric design around them had been repaired. With the weeding done and the vineyard beyond the gardens in flower, the sight would be glorious to his parents, who were coming home from the treatment center today.

They were back together.

It was hard to believe four weeks had passed since Max had followed Andrea into the cottage and discovered his father passed out on the couch. During the time the two of them had been in therapy with Dr. Shand, Max had worked nonstop to get the estate ready for them.

Not everything was done yet, but it didn't matter. They would see that the main house had not only been painted inside and out, the entire front had been remodeled according to the plans his father had envisioned years ago—before the strife in their marriage had torn their lives apart.

The vaulted ceiling with heavy beams set off tall glass windows and doors opening out to the garden via the extensive slate deck. Max had brought in stonemasons to build a half wall around the trellis-covered amphitheater where people could sit, connecting it to the deck at the far end of the house.

While one team of gardeners had espaliered the wisteria and bougainvillea vines over the latticework, another had cleaned up the grounds around the side of the house reserved for guest parking. Max had done a massive amount of weeding, and now the new flower plantings brought the winery to life.

All this was good. So far the multitasking had saved his life. Since the day Andrea had bolted out of the shed in pain, he'd seen next to nothing of her except from the roof, where he was repairing shingles, or from an upstairs window he was washing.

Before Max told his father why he'd fired Jim, he'd had a talk with Dr. Shand about the scene in the shed. The psychiatrist had advised Max to leave Andrea alone for a while. She needed to get in touch with her feelings and gain a different perspective. That would take some time. Later he could go to her, when she'd had an opportunity to heal. Maybe she would come to him. But Max should be patient. He had never needed her more, but he'd decided to follow the doctor's counsel.

This morning he locked the back door and started down the steps. Andrea's car was gone. She must have already left for a business appointment. In a few days, when the painters were ready to start on the cottage, he would take her to his penthouse in San Francisco and they'd talk until she came willingly into his arms.

Before he reached his car he heard the phone signal that he had voice mail. The construction foreman often called him with a question before he even arrived for work. It must have come in while he was showering. Max pulled it out of his pocket to retrieve the message.

"Hi, Max. It's Andrea. I'm impressed with all the work you've done so far. The place looks fabulous. Your father will be so thrilled. I talked to Dr. Shand last night. He told me your parents are coming home today. That's the best news in the world.

"Just so you know, I've rented a place in Napa, where I've opened a small studio and gallery. I also rented an apartment. Last week the moving van loaded all my things from the cottage. You weren't here or I would have said goodbye in person.

"As of yesterday it's all cleaned up, so you can do what you want with it. The door's locked. I left the keys on the kitchen counter. Steve will have extras. I would have brought them to you yesterday, but I assumed you were at the treatment center.

"Please don't think I've left your parents in the lurch. I've arranged for a housekeeper from St. Helena to come in whenever Steve wants. I've left her phone number on the counter with the keys. She comes highly recommended by friends of mine and will be great in the wine tasting room because she has worked in several before.

"Tell your parents that when I have my grand opening, I'll invite all of you. As you know, I wouldn't be where I am today without your father. Tell him that for me. Thanks and happy reunion!"

Like the heavy stone slab that had fallen off one of the trucks last week, Max's heart plummeted to his feet, sending the grist flying.

Chapter Eight

After the aides put Andrea's aunt in the wheelchair, she pushed her out to the covered patio to enjoy the warm, fresh air. No one else had come out here yet. The pots of purple and pink petunias were a welcome sight. Her aunt's pneumonia seemed to be hanging on, even with the help of oxygen. Maybe the flowers would give her spirits a boost.

Andrea pulled up one of the patio chairs next to her and sat down. Though her aunt never spoke and didn't know her, she grasped her hand and held it. "I'm sorry you're so sick. I wish I knew how to help you."

Right now Andrea's life was a desert. Already she couldn't stand her new second-floor apartment, which felt enclosed after the open spaces on the Roussillac winery. The only thing going for it was that it was within walking distance of the small studio Nancy had found for her.

By now Andrea would have thought Max might call and ask her to see him again, if only to continue where they'd left off, but it hadn't happened. Leaving the vineyard had been the hardest but wisest thing she'd ever done. It was past time to free herself from him.

"Oh, Aunt Edna…" She pressed her aunt's hand to her hot cheek. "You know that phone call from Sammi I've been waiting for since I moved to Napa? Well, it has never come." The tears started again. "She hasn't forgiven me. She never will. When I e-mailed her about the move, I promised that the same room she'd had at the cottage had been recreated at the apartment and was waiting for her.

"She e-mailed me back this morning. There was no mention of her coming home. All she said was that she was finishing up an unexpected assignment in the Maldives, then flying straight to Alaska. I should have contacted Chris's parents and told them everything. I'm afraid I've really lost my daughter. The damage I did was too great. I'm the worst mother who ever lived."

The tears kept coming. Andrea tried to stifle them when a family she recognized came outside, pushing their grandfather in a wheelchair. They nodded in her direction.

She squeezed her aunt's hand before putting it back on her lap. "You know what? You need to lie down. We've been out here long enough. I'm afraid I have to go." She turned the wheelchair around and took her back to her room.

"Tomorrow's my grand opening. It's not a very big gallery, nothing elegant to compete with others in the area, but at least my paintings have been uncrated and are on display. I'll see you the day after tomorrow and tell you all about it."

She kissed her aunt's cheek, then found Judy in the hall to let her know Edna was back in her room. With the promise to return, she hurried out to the car.

Brad Warshaw had asked her to lunch and would be coming by the studio for her in an hour. That barely gave her enough time to make it back to Napa. Since she'd been setting up her new studio and gallery, she'd seen quite a lot of him. While she worked in the back room, producing the tiles needed for the Casa Bonita, he'd insisted on helping hang her paintings.

His designer's eye had made the best use of the space and Andrea was very grateful for his help and his company. It kept thoughts of Sammi and Max at bay.

When she'd called Steve to invite him to the opening, he had put Helen on the phone, and the three of them were able to say what was in their hearts. Andrea found out Max had gone back to San Francisco to deal with important banking business he'd left too long. She had asked them to extend an invitation to their son.

She heard happiness in their voices. If she had done one thing right in her life, it was to make that phone call to Max telling him his father needed him. Since then a miracle had happened to the de Roussillac family.

Would that one could be granted to her and Sammi, but Andrea held out little hope. For that to happen she needed to have been a different kind of mother from the beginning. Somehow she just kept making things worse.

To add to her pain, Max was well and truly out of her life.

AT FIVE TO SEVEN Saturday evening, Max found a parking place and headed for Andrea's studio, where he'd arranged to meet his parents. According to them, she planned to keep the gallery open until eight. He'd waited until now to drive up from San Francisco.

Once the showing was over and she'd closed the doors, he had plans for them. They were going to talk everything out until he wrung a confession of love from her.

He rounded the corner to the address his father had given him, but didn't see his parents' car there. They'd had another therapy session earlier in the day. Maybe they'd been delayed.

As he spotted the gallery, his adrenaline kicked in. He hadn't been with Andrea in weeks and ached for her. A nice crowd of people milled about, studying the paintings, Max saw as he entered. He noted with satisfaction that the blue hydrangeas he'd sent were prominently displayed among the many floral offerings sent by friends and business associates. Where was she?

As he looked around, he spotted her redheaded friend studying one of the paintings. He strolled over to her. "Good evening, Nancy. Could you tell me where to find Andrea?"

She turned sober eyes on him. "Oh, Max—it's so sad. I'm afraid she had to leave."

"During the opening of her gallery?" He knew he sounded terse, but his disappointment was so great he couldn't help it.

"There was an emergency."

"Samantha?"

"No. About an hour ago she received a call from the nursing home. Her aunt just passed away."

Max felt as if he'd been punched in the gut. "I'm going to go find her." He turned and strode swiftly out the door. The second he reached his car he called his father. "Where are you, Dad?"

"Five minutes away. Sorry we're late. It couldn't be helped. What about you?"

"On my way to Rutherford. During the showing, Andrea got a call from the nursing home. Edna passed away this evening."

His father made a sound in his throat. "It's a blessing, but it's still going to be very hard on Andrea for a while, especially with Samantha gone."

"I know. I'm leaving to find her right now."

"That's good. She's going to need you. Who's minding the gallery?"

"Nancy Owens. There's still a crowd."

"I'm glad to hear it. Tell Andrea we'll stay to help until the showing's over, and make certain everything gets locked up tight."

"She'll be grateful for that."

"When you see her, give her our love and tell her we're at her disposal to help plan the funeral arrangements. Samantha will have to be notified."

"I would imagine Andrea has already phoned her."

"Since their falling out I'm afraid little Sammi hasn't made it easy for her mother to talk to her. Let's hope she'll at least e-mail Andrea back. If she's trying to punish her by not getting back to her, that would really tear Andrea up."

"Do you think Samantha would be that vindictive?"

"Let's just say I don't *want* to think it."

"Neither do I," Max said in a haunted whisper. "I'll talk to you later."

The rest of the drive passed in a blur. To his alarm he didn't see Andrea's car when he pulled into the nursing-home parking lot. He rushed inside to Reception. The night manager came to the desk. "Can I help you?"

"I've come to see Andrea Danbury. I understand her aunt, Edna Green, passed away this evening."

"That's right. Ms. Danbury was here to take care of things, then she left."

Max closed his eyes for a moment. He must have just missed her. "Alone?"

"No. She was with a friend."

He wanted to ask if the person were male or female, but caught himself in time. "Thank you very much."

Once back in the car, he phoned his father again. "I got here too late. What's the address of her apartment in Napa? I'm going to drive back and see if I can't catch up to her."

After his father gave it to him, he thanked him and

headed off again. Though Max drove over the speed limit, it seemed to take forever to reach Napa. Using the car's guidance system, he found her three-story apartment building without a problem.

In seconds he spotted her car in one of the stalls, but that didn't mean she was home. Then he saw a familiar-looking Audi in the guest parking area and ground his teeth. Andrea's companion would have to handle another interruption, because Max needed to see her.

When she opened the door, he saw Brad Warshaw seated on the couch across the room behind her. "Andrea— I got here as soon as I could."

She looked shocked to see him. "You heard about Aunt Edna?"

"Nancy told me. I drove to the nursing home to be with you, but the manager said you'd just left. I was worried about you."

He noticed she was clinging to the door handle. "I really do appreciate your concern, Max, but I'm not alone. Brad brought me home."

"So I see." He had to rein in his emotions. "I'm glad you have someone with you at a time like this. Is Samantha on her way home for the funeral?"

"I'm not sure. I phoned the Hilton in Male, where she's staying, but I had to leave a message."

"Male?" he questioned. "As in the Maldives?"

"Yes."

Good grief. There'd been a tsunami in that part of the world a few days ago, but with her gallery opening, Andrea must not have been listening to the news. "I thought she'd be in Alaska by now."

"I thought so, too, but I had an e-mail from her recently. She said she and her crew had been given a short assignment in Male after leaving Thailand, so she had to put off her flight to Alaska for a few more days."

No matter what, Samantha loved her aunt. If she hadn't answered Andrea yet it meant she couldn't! The hairs stood up on the back of Max's neck.

"I hope she gets in touch with you soon. If there's anything I can do for you, call me. Mom and Dad are at the gallery to keep an eye on everything. They'll close up for you."

"That's very generous of them. Nancy and Pete said they'd do it."

"I'm sure the four of them will work things out. They send their love and want to help with the funeral arrangements. If you'd like it to be at the vineyard, all you have to do is say so."

Andrea smoothed the hair off her forehead in a nervous gesture. "Thank you for the offer, but before Aunt Edna got Alzheimer's, she said she wanted a graveside service near my parents' in Rutherford. There won't be very many people. I prefer to keep it simple."

She looked shaken. She needed her daughter. Max wanted to hold her in his arms and never let her go. "You're exhausted, Andrea. After such a traumatic evening you need rest. I'll say good-night."

"Good night. Thank you for coming, Max."

Once the door closed, he raced back to his car and phoned his father. "Dad? I've just been with Andrea at her apartment. "

"How is she?"

"Holding on. She was with Brad Warshaw, a designer she's obviously been seeing. The point is, she hasn't heard from Samantha. I think I know why." When he told his father the reason for his concern, Steve was equally alarmed.

"I'm going to fly to Male tonight on the corporate jet

and bring her home if I can, but I probably won't make it back in time for the funeral. Tell Andrea why. She said Edna wanted a simple graveside service."

"Helen and I will help her. You go and find her precious Sammi."

Two hours later, Max was sitting in the club compartment of the jet. He immersed himself in half a dozen Pacific Rim newspapers he'd bought before taking off. He felt a chill when he read the latest information on the Maldives.

Following the Indian Ocean earthquake, the Maldives were devastated by a tsunami. Only nine islands were reported to have escaped flooding, while fifty-seven faced serious damage to critical infrastructure, fourteen had to be totally evacuated and six were decimated.

A further twenty-one island resorts were forced to shut down due to serious damage. The total destruction has been estimated at over $400 million. The brutal impact of the waves on the low-lying islands was mitigated by the fact there was no continental shelf or land mass to slow the force of the water. The tallest waves were reported to be fourteen feet high.

Max's heart felt as if it had been squeezed with an iron hand.

ANDREA WISHED she could have invited Max inside, but not while Brad was with her. Since she'd closed the door, there'd been a lot of phone calls. Word had spread. It seemed everyone she'd ever known had phoned to offer sympathy and ask what they could do to help. She was very touched by the outpouring, but had the insane desire to call Max and beg him to come back.

"Andrea?" Brad murmured. "I can tell you're so tired you could drop. With the buildup to the gallery opening and now this, it's been an emotional day for you. I should go."

Brad didn't want to leave. She knew he was waiting for her to ask him to stay. Maybe if Max hadn't come… Seeing him again had upset her so much she was drained.

"Perhaps it would be better. You've put in long hours, too, and I'm so grateful."

Her words left him no choice but to walk to the door. Andrea followed him, saying, "Thank you so much for everything. You've been wonderful. I don't know what I would have done without you."

"That's nice to hear." Surprising her, he leaned forward and kissed her briefly on the lips for the first time.

Andrea sensed he wanted a response, but she couldn't give him one. Not because of her grief. It was because she feared he was trying to compete with Max, who'd brought his masculine energy with him.

"I'll call you tomorrow," Brad promised.

"Please do." She pecked him on the cheek before he left. After locking the door, she got ready for bed and pretty well collapsed after climbing under the covers, but her mind wouldn't turn off.

She'd lost her aunt and possibly her daughter. Tears trickled out of her eyes. She turned on her stomach.

I need you, Max.

ON TUESDAY, SHE FOUND herself thinking the same thing as she stepped out of the limo at the cemetery. The hearse had arrived ahead of it. Steve and Helen were waiting for her and gave her long hugs.

Cars lined both sides of the narrow laneway. Beneath the canopy provided, a surprisingly large crowd of her friends, including Brad, had assembled.

But Max wasn't there, and no Sammi.... *Not even a word from her.*

Shattered at the thought, Andrea sat there numbly as the minister wrapped an arm around her shoulders. Then he took his place at the end of the pale blue casket, Steve and Helen's contribution. On top lay a gorgeous spray of pink roses. She'd seen the flowers at the mortuary. Max had sent them. *Where is he?*

Andrea stared dry-eyed at the casket holding her aunt's body. She'd dressed her in a beautiful white gown with lace at the neck and sleeves. Her great-aunt Edna was at peace now, thank heaven. The moment was surreal as the minister delivered his talk and gave the graveside prayer, committing her into the hands of the Almighty.

As she finally turned away, Steve put his arm around her. "Max couldn't be here because he's gone to the Maldives to find Sammi."

"You're kidding...."

"No. He knows you need her."

I need them both.

Chapter Nine

Samantha was still registered at the Hilton, but from staff frantically trying to locate people, Max found out she was among the missing. He'd been praying nonstop that wherever she'd gone to take photographs, she'd survived the tidal wave. If she wasn't found, Andrea would never be the same again.

After twenty hours of torturous waiting at the Male airport, Max saw more shell-shocked people climb out of the latest rescue helicopter. The ones who couldn't walk were put on stretchers.

When Samantha didn't appear, he walked to the next landing pad, where a military helicopter was coming in. Maybe this would be the one that held her. This was the plight of thousands. The Red Cross was overwhelmed with requests, Max's among them.

A local woman and her child were helped off. Next came a sight that filled him with joy. It had been ages since he'd seen Samantha. Despite the fact that she looked drawn and exhausted, he hadn't realized she'd grown into such a beautiful young woman.

The golden-blond hair that used to cascade halfway down her back now hung in a limp braid. Her cotton top looked stained, her khaki pants were wrinkled and torn, but she was alive. She could move on her own steam and he could return her to Andrea in one piece.

He moved toward her. "Samantha? Over here!"

She swung her head around. "Max?" A strange expression broke out on her face. "What are you doing here?"

Her response wasn't warm or chilly, but in between. It prevented him from hugging her. "If you're not too weak to walk, let's go back to your hotel and I'll explain on the way."

"I promised to wait here for the guys. They'll be coming in on one of the other helicopters."

"Then I'll wait with you."

They moved a short distance away. She eyed him warily. "How come you're in Male?"

"When you didn't return your mother's phone call, I got worried and flew here to find out why."

"Why would you do that?"

He took a calming breath. "Because your aunt Edna passed away at the same time the tsunami struck."

"What?" Her blue eyes darkened. "She's dead?"

"Yes. There was a graveside service for her day before yesterday. My parents helped your mom take care of things."

She looked shocked. "Your parents—"

"Yes. They're back together again and are planning to get remarried as soon as possible."

Tears glazed Sammi's eyes, but not one fell. "I would have come home if I'd known, but our boat was forced ashore on one of the islands. I lost all my things, including my cell phone. We were stuck there in chest-deep water for two days, until help came a little while ago."

"What a horrible ordeal. Thank God you're alive. I've been watching every flight that's come in. Here." He held out his cell phone. "Call your mom and let her know you're alive and safe with me."

She stared at it for a minute, but didn't take it. "I'd rather call her when I get back to the hotel. I still don't understand why *you* came."

Max cocked his head. "I think you do. I think you know I've been in love with your mother since the day I met her. Why else would I have remained single all these years? I want to marry her, but she doesn't know that yet."

Samantha averted her eyes.

"Whatever affects her, affects me. Since she loves you more than life itself, I knew that losing you would kill her. That's why I'm here. To fly you home. Your mom needs you right now."

He could see Samantha was having a real struggle within herself. "Sammi? Has she e-mailed you about what's been going on at the vineyard since you left for Vietnam?"

"She's written some," the girl replied reluctantly, "but only to tell me she moved to Napa and was opening a gallery."

Evidently Samantha hadn't given her mother a chance to explain anything. "Then she didn't tell you about Jim."

Her eyes lifted to his. "What about him?"

"I fired him."

"Good. Why didn't Steve do it?"

"Because I've been running the vineyard while he's been in an alcohol treatment center, getting his life back together."

After a long silence Max heard her whisper she was glad. "Did you know Jim had the hots for your mother?" Sammi added. "Steve never seemed to notice how he looked at Helen."

"No." But with that bit of information Max was able to fit the last piece into the puzzle.

"Jim was a creep, but you haven't been around lately to notice."

"That's true, but there were reasons." For the next little

while Max related everything that had happened up to and including the incident in the shed that day. A stillness surrounded Samantha when he'd finished.

"Did you hear what I just told you?" he asked her.

"Yes, and I'm really glad for all of you that everything has worked out so well. If Mother wants to marry you, then you both have my blessing, but in the meantime you don't have to wait around here for me. As soon as I can say goodbye to the guys, I'm getting on the next flight to Alaska."

"In that case let me fly you there in my plane."

"No, thank you. This is something I want to do myself."

The old saying that butter wouldn't melt in her mouth applied here. "I hope for your sake and your mother's that one day you'll soften toward her and forgive her. None of us is perfect."

"That's true. If I were more perfect, I'd probably be able to."

Max pulled five one-hundred-dollar bills from his wallet and stuffed them in her shirt pocket. "Pretend that's a gift from your father. I'm sure he's thrilled that you want to meet his family. Just remember that when you were a little golden cherub, I fell in love with *you* as well as your mother. God bless you in your quest, Samantha."

He kissed her cheek before walking away. After he boarded his plane, he phoned Andrea. All he got was her voice mail.

Brad Warshaw wouldn't have left her alone after the funeral, but that didn't matter. Max's message was guaranteed to grab her attention.

ANDREA WAS OUT OF THE shower and drying her hair when she heard the sound on her phone. Someone had called and left a voice mail. She hurried over to the dresser to reach for it and clicked on.

"Andrea? I've just been with Samantha and am on my way home from the Maldives. You may already have heard from her. When she tells you about her adventure, you'll understand why she couldn't make it home for the service. I offered to bring her home on my plane, but she has other plans. Before I left her, she promised to call you as soon as she returned to the hotel. As for you and me, we have to talk. Don't go to work in the morning. After I land in San Francisco, I'll drive to Napa, and should be at your apartment by ten."

While Andrea reeled with joy because her daughter was all right and Max was on his way home to see her, her phone rang. This had to be Sammi!

She clicked on. "Hello?"

"Hi, Mom." That subdued voice…

"Oh, Sammi!" she cried. "Oh, honey—I'm so happy to hear from you and know you're all right. I just received a voice mail from Max. He said he found you in Male."

"Yup. He was there when I got off the helicopter. I heard Aunty Ed died. I'm sorry I couldn't be there. Was she in pain?" Her voice trembled.

"The doctor assured me she died of the pneumonia in her sleep, with no struggle."

"That's good."

"Yes. It was a lovely graveside service. The flowers were gorgeous. She would have been pleased."

"I'm sure she's happy now." After a hesitation Sammi said, "Max told me Steve and Helen are getting married again."

"That's right. It's wonderful."

"I'm glad he fired Jim."

"So am I. I've missed talking to you about everything, but first I want to know what happened to you."

"Two days ago the small motorboat the guys and I were in capsized, and we were stranded on one of the islands. We had to wait it out till help came."

"Thank heaven it did!"

"Yeah. We lost all our equipment and phones in the tidal wave. Luckily, the magazine will reimburse us. I'm staying at the hotel until I arrange my flight to Alaska. It's already been paid for."

There was no persuading Sammi to come home first. "I'll wire you some money to help get you through. How much do you need?"

"Max gave me five hundred dollars. I'll be fine. Tell him I'll pay him back with my next paycheck."

Andrea's eyes closed tightly. She loved him so much. "I'll tell him. Honey?"

"I can't talk any longer, Mom. Other people need to use the hotel phone. We're lined up here. I'll e-mail you when I get to Alaska. Bye for now."

More bittersweet tears trickled out of Andrea's eyes. Her daughter was safe, but she wouldn't be coming home.

Andrea replayed Max's message several times simply to hear the sound of his voice again. When he hadn't shown up at the cemetery the other day, she'd hardly been able to bear it. Naturally, Brad had picked up on that. Later that night, after he'd brought her home from the dinner Nancy had given, he'd confronted her.

"You're in love with Max, aren't you." It wasn't a question.

She couldn't lie to him. "Yes, but we've never had a normal relationship."

"Well, something's going on. When the two of you are together, it's like no one else exists for you."

No one else does.

"I'm so sorry, Brad."

"Don't be. It's life, but since I can't fight it, I'm going to do the smart thing and move on. Rest assured our professional relationship will remain intact."

She bowed her head. "You're a wonderful man," she whispered.

"But he's the lucky one," he'd whispered back, giving her arm a squeeze before he left.

Andrea let out a tormented sigh. She'd been alone in this claustrophobic apartment all night, waiting in agony for Max, not knowing what to expect when he did arrive.

She'd already changed clothes three times before deciding on a plum-colored blouson top and white skirt, something in between dressy and casual. After putting on lipstick and a little blusher to cover up her washed-out look, she glanced at her watch again. It was almost ten-thirty. A delayed flight might mean hours more waiting.

At quarter to eleven her cell phone rang. She grabbed it and saw that it was Max. "H-hello?"

"Andrea—sorry I'm late. To save time, meet me down in the parking lot." *What did he mean, 'save time'?* "My limo should be there any minute." He hung up before she could reply.

His urgent tone had her hurrying into the kitchen for her purse, then rushing out of the apartment. As she descended the last flight of steps she saw a black limo turn in to the parking area and come to a stop.

The rear door opened. Max's dark head appeared. "Come and get in, Andrea." His compelling voice had her scrambling inside. He closed the door.

"What's going on?"

While he smoothed a strand of hair away from her

cheek, his black eyes burned with heat, creating a different kind of tension inside her.

"We have to get to the Napa Valley airport as soon as possible."

"Why?"

"Because we're on our way to a wedding in Reno that's going to be taking place at the civil registry in about two hours."

Her thoughts reeled. "Whose wedding?"

Max slid her onto his lap so she was half lying in his arms. *"Ours."* His mouth muffled the cry that escaped her throat. "I told Samantha I was going to marry you and she gave us her blessing."

"She did?"

"She knows I've loved you with a terrible hunger for so many years, I can't wait another second to make you my wife."

Maybe she was dreaming. Maybe not. The kiss he was giving her was a husband's kiss, hot with desire. "Will you marry me, darling?" The hint of vulnerability was still there in his eyes and voice. It took her back to those early years when she'd continually turned him down.

Andrea caught his face between her hands. "Yes! It's what I've wanted for more years than I care to remember. I'm so in love with you. I need to be able to love you day and night for the rest of our lives or there's no point to this existence." She clutched him tighter.

After telling the limo driver to head for the airport, Max focused solely on Andrea. Time ceased to exist while they exchanged one fiery kiss after another, trying to catch up on the years they'd lost. Andrea never wanted this ecstasy to stop.

He eventually buried his face in her hair. "You have no idea the fantasies I've had about you."

"I think I do. One of mine has been to have *your* baby."

His breath caught. "At your age there are too many risks. I wouldn't ask that of you. I couldn't bear to lose you now."

"Max, I know several women who've had babies past forty and everything went fine. The truth is, I want to have another child, your child. There's no reason we shouldn't try. You'll make the best father. Can't you see a new little de Roussillac running around the vineyard?"

"You really mean it?" he cried with joy in his voice. Andrea didn't think she'd ever heard him sound like that before.

"I'm marrying you in a little while, aren't I? How much more proof do you need?"

His eyes burned like fire as he gazed at her. "If we're going to try for a family, then it's settled, I'm retiring from the bank. Papa needs me to help him run the vineyard."

Andrea threw her arms around Max's neck, too overcome with happiness to talk.

"We'll gut the cottage and remodel it with bigger rooms and a sunny loft you can use for your workspace." He gently bit her earlobe. "One of my fantasies was to live there with you and make love to you all day long while we listened to *Tosca*."

"I didn't know you liked opera."

"You know something?" he murmured against her lips. "As well as we think we know each other, there's still so much to discover, we'll need a lifetime of loving to learn it all."

"Sir," said a voice over the speaker. "We've arrived at the airport."

Max crushed Andrea against him. "This is it. Are you ready?"

"I've been ready since the first time you walked into the

tasting room with Steve. I remember thinking that if I could get that gorgeous, intelligent, fabulous man to love me, I'd be the luckiest woman on earth."

A deep groan came out of him. "When I think of the time we've wasted…"

"We can't afford to look back. All that matters is that we're finally together, where we belong. I love you, Max de Roussillac. I *love* you."

JULY HAD COME TO THE vineyard. Max figured it was at least seventy degrees this morning. Perfect weather, but then every day—every night—was perfect since he'd married Andrea. There were moments when he was afraid he might die from too much happiness.

"Have you heard anything I've said?" his father teased.

Max grinned at him. They'd been out inspecting a section of the vineyard that needed to be replanted. "I have, and with all our work, it's my opinion we'll see a much higher crop yield next year."

"I was asking you how soon you plan to take Andrea on that overdue honeymoon to Alsace." His father winked.

"We're not in any hurry," he murmured. For the last three weeks their lives had been a continuous honeymoon. He hadn't been able to sell his penthouse fast enough and leave the emptiness of his former world behind. Everything he'd ever wanted was right here with the woman who made him feel immortal.

"What have you heard from Sammi?"

"Just that she and the other photographers picked up more equipment and have been filming the aftermath of the tsunami for their magazine."

The only cloud on his horizon was his wife's heartache over her daughter, who continued to remain out of reach physically and emotionally. That was the one area no one but God could rectify.

"If I know my little Sammi, one of these days she'll come around. Andrea just has to give it more time. Luckily, she has you now."

"She does, and I promised I'd be home for lunch."

"Your mother has mine waiting, too. Let's go."

They walked between the rows of vines. When they reached the road and came within view of the cottage, Max patted his father's shoulder before heading inside. The second he found Andrea, he swept her into his arms and carried her through the partially renovated house to their bedroom.

He stared into her eyes. "Do you have any idea how beautiful you are?"

"I was just going to tell you the same thing. I love you so much it hurts."

"Then let me take away your pain."

He lowered her to the covers and followed her down. Though it had only been a few hours since the sun had come up over the vineyard and he'd made love to her, he couldn't wait any longer to kiss her senseless again. His wife was always waiting for him, giving him so much more than he'd ever thought possible.

It was midafternoon when he rolled her on top of him, temporarily sated. "After we eat, was there anything special you wanted to do with the rest of this day, you gorgeous creature?"

A mysterious smile lit up her face. "As a matter of fact, there is something."

He kissed her luscious mouth. "Don't keep me in suspense."

"You know the little shop over at Kent Place that sells unfinished handmade reproductions of nineteenth-century furniture?"

"Yes?"

"Well, there's this adorable hutch and crib I'd like you to look at. I thought I'd paint them an antique blue and add some nursery rhyme figures."

"Sure, and after that we'll—" But he didn't finish the sentence. In the next breath his hands stilled on her back. "Andrea?"

"I have no idea if we're going to have a baby or not. It's too early to tell, but I thought it wouldn't hurt to plan ahead just in case."

His heart was too full to talk. All he could do was kiss her again.

The next morning the baby furniture arrived at the cottage. The deliverymen carried everything into the studio. Andrea couldn't wait to get to work painting them. Hopefully, one day soon she would discover she was pregnant. A baby brought so much joy. She wanted Max to have the full experience. She wanted him to be totally happy because he'd literally become her life.

Speaking of her husband, he'd be arriving from the vineyard for lunch in a minute. She'd better get it ready, but first she checked her e-mails and saw one from Sammi.

Hey, Mom—

I'm finally here in Ketchikan. Ever since I found Dad's journal, I've been trying to imagine how I would feel once I entered the world he grew up in.

I know this sounds weird, but for the first time in my life I feel I'm at home. That probably sounds crazy. Never mind—it must be all the sleep deprivation and climate changes. That unexpected photo shoot in the Maldives may win our team a cover.

Since there are no flights that I can afford out to

Prince of Wales Island, I'll have to wait to take a ferry ride tomorrow. I'm staying the night at the Grizzly Inn. I hate having to wait another day to see if I have grandparents who are alive. I still can't believe I'm saying that! Grandparents—like a normal person...

Well, you know how to reach me.

While Andrea was pondering this latest message, she heard sounds from the front of the house, then felt Max's arms go around her. Over her shoulder he read the e-mail, then kissed her neck. "Are you all right?"

"I am now that you're here."

He pressed his face in her silky hair. "Don't be afraid. After the miracle that has happened to us, I know the day will come when Samantha's heart is softened and you get her back. In the meantime, I hope we're granted a long, long life together, Andrea, because we've only just begun to live."

"Hold me, darling," she cried softly. "Never let me go."

"You can say that to me after the way I've hung around you all these years?"

Her breathing had grown shallow. "You know what I mean."

"I'm not sure that I do," he teased. "Maybe you'd better show me."

* * * * *

A DAUGHTER'S DISCOVERY
Dominique Burton

For my mother, who always believed in me;
to Dave for all of your help;
and to Victoria Merritt at the Craig, Alaska,
Parks and Recreation Department,
for answering all my questions.

Chapter One

Samantha Danbury breathed in the smells of pine and wet earth that hung in the cool Alaskan night air. She'd spent the last three hours walking around Ketchikan to find a hotel that had a vacancy for the first week of July. When she entered the well-kept motel room with its bearskin rug and rustic wood furniture, she let out a sigh of relief.

After placing her camera case on the table, she plopped her enormous backpack full of clothes and toiletries on the chair beside her. She arched her back, working out the kinks that had formed after a long day of travel.

The room had an immense canopy bed made of pine that looked incredibly inviting. Except for the hotel in Male, the capital of the Maldives, she'd spent most of the last two months in Southeast Asia, living out of grungy hotels or a tent.

Sammi couldn't resist jumping onto the puffy bedding. The down comforter swallowed her up, making her want to fall asleep. Unfortunately, there were two things she had to do before that could happen. E-mail her mom and eat.

Slowly, Sammi sat up, running her fingers through her straight blond hair. She fumbled for her purse and grabbed an elastic to put it in a braid. She also took out a protein bar to stop her stomach from grumbling.

Her feet became painfully alive with pins and needles as soon as they were elevated. To get the blood flowing, she kicked off her all-terrain boots, got off the bed and walked around the room until the pain subsided.

She stopped, turning her gaze to her backpack, which contained the journal. To her sorrow, its existence had caused a rift between her and her mother she feared might be too big to overcome. Even though it had been only a few months since they'd fought, it felt like a year. Now Aunty Ed had passed away, too.

Waves of loneliness threatened to consume Samantha. She knew it was for the best that her aunt was out of her misery. But to never see her again...

Sammi closed her eyes, trying to shut out the horror of the last few weeks. How could she complain about an aunt who'd died peacefully when thousands of people had lost loved ones? Her latest assignment had her photographing faces against a landscape left desolate by a tsunami—an experience she hoped never to repeat. In fact, she never wanted to cover a disaster again.

Realizing she was hovering over her luggage, she reached for the key in her jean pocket to open the special latch on her backpack. Once she'd retrieved the journal, she sat down and opened it.

Her fingers shook. The doctor had warned her about the aftermath of living through a disaster. She'd been so busy with the crew at the time, capturing every shot she could. Now all she could think of was how many of those survivors hadn't been able to salvage a memento of their father or mother like this.

How could you have kept this from me for all these years, Mom?

The brown diary was large enough to hold pictures, but

not too bulky. All her life she'd longed to know her father. Had he loved her? What kind of man had he been? Where was he from? Did he have a family? Had he loved her mother?

In the worn pages she'd found the answers. She would never have known any of this if she hadn't discovered his backpack in one of the closets at home on the vineyard in St. Helena, California.

Her father, Chris Engstrom, had been born and raised in the tiny town of Craig, Alaska. From the pictures, it looked like he came from a loving family, with two older brothers and parents. Sammi was convinced that pictures didn't lie. As a professional photographer, she could read body language and gestures. The way people held themselves in candid poses showed a lot about them.

What had happened to make her father run away from home?

He'd been a prop airplane pilot, with blue eyes, blond hair and an adventurous soul, and he'd wanted to see the world. "Just like me," Sammi whispered.

At thirty-two years of age he was passing through the Napa Valley of California when he'd met her mom, Andrea Danbury, a seventeen-year-old, ash-blond beauty working at a restaurant in Rutherford. It was a whirlwind romance that ended up with a pregnant Andrea and Chris living together with Aunty Ed. Just a couple of months after they'd found out about the baby, his plane went down and his body was never recovered.

Sammi had known her father was a wanderer and a pilot, but she'd been told nothing else. She'd learned he sent money home to his family in Alaska with every paycheck he earned, but she didn't know why.

Her mother claimed that she'd been so hurt Chris hadn't loved her enough to tell his family about them, she'd never said a word to Sammi about his parents. They'd been kept a secret from her for twenty-three years.

But *was* her mom to blame for all this?

Sammi had come to Alaska to find out if her grandparents were alive or not. Either way, she would be able to put this chapter of her life to rest. There was a part of her that needed to see where her dad was from, where he'd grown up. She wanted to talk to some people who'd known him and could tell her how he'd lived. If by any chance her grandparents were alive, then she would do all she could to get to know them.

She picked up her birth certificate, which had slipped out of the journal, then set her laptop on the bed. Once she'd put in her wireless Internet card, she grabbed her snack and began eating again.

While waiting for the computer to boot up, Sammi stepped over to the window and peered out at the magical green world of Alaska, where the land, ocean, clouds and sky seemed to go on forever.

Eventually she looked at the clock on the nightstand. It was 10:00 p.m. and the sun was just setting. She finally closed the curtains, then headed back to the bed to send her mother an e-mail before going to sleep.

THE NEXT AFTERNOON Sammi watched the colorful town of Ketchikan shrink into the distance from the small ferry boat. The place bustled with tourists and traffic. She couldn't believe her luck in finding a local ferry with a captain willing to take her over to Prince of Wales Island for twenty extra dollars.

She'd decided to come up to Ketchikan on a whim, not realizing it was the height of the tourist season and most lodgings were booked, unless you had lots of money. The one thing she didn't have.

No matter. Focusing on the negative would do her little good now. She was here and the views were awe inspiring. For the next hour Sammi was caught up in shooting pictures of humpback whales, bald eagles and picturesque green islands with seals sunning themselves on the shore.

She turned her face to the wind. The taste of salt was delicious, but the weather was chilly, since the sun had decided to hide behind the clouds. The once-blue water had turned a grayish hue. It made Sammi feel oddly peaceful as the boat continued its three-hour journey to the port town of Hollis.

Since the rest of the ferry was used for local and government vehicles commuting to the island, the only place to warm up was in the captain's quarters. She ventured inside.

JAKE POWELL ENJOYED the peace of the three-hour ferry ride home to Prince of Wales Island. He fiddled with his iPod and its converter in the music deck of his truck, searching for a song, and looked up at the vistas of never ending sky and water. The beauty of Alaska always amazed him. This was God's country, a place he'd taken an oath to protect as chief ranger of the Tongass National Park.

He took his hat off and ran a hand through his dark curls, noting that dust and dirt fell out as he massaged his scalp. *Time for a shower!*

It had been a long couple of days trying to stop some poachers down in the Misty Fjords National Monument. A smile crossed his face when he thought of them spending the Fourth of July weekend in jail.

The Fourth of July.

That meant his brother, C.J., would be at their parents'

home for his annual visit. His appearance usually sent Jake out of the room. He turned up the volume on the song playing.

Jake did his best to be gone when C.J. came to Craig, but he'd promised his mom he'd come to the family's Fourth of July barbecue this year, and he was a man of his word.

He and his brother had been the best of friends growing up. Now he wondered how on earth twins could look so much alike, yet be such polar opposites.

It had been thirteen years since Jake had asked Lisa Meyers to marry him, on the night of their high school graduation. He'd thought she'd loved him. He would never forget the shock when she'd said she loved C.J., that he was exciting and fun. In a scornful voice, she'd told Jake he was boring, serious and already old.

Lisa's family had moved to Craig when she was seven. Ever since then Jake had been in love with her. They'd dated from their junior year on. His brother's betrayal had been so great, he'd put up a wall between them Jake had never cared to breach.

To C.J., life was all fun and games. Women came and went out of his life. Not able to get out of Alaska fast enough, he'd moved to San Francisco at age eighteen, and in time became a fireman, loving the big-city life.

Jake hadn't needed to go away to find himself. He had everything a man could want right here—a house, family and a great job....

The sound of his cell phone ringing interrupted his thoughts. Who was calling?

He picked up the phone, looked at the caller ID and grimaced. *Emily.* He chucked the phone back on the seat and grabbed some jerky instead.

It's over. Told her that two weeks ago. The only lady in my heart is a hundred-pound furry rottweiler named

*Beastly. C.J. better be ready. I'm in no mood to deal with
poachers intruding on my territory.*

"HI, CAPTAIN LOVELL."

The short, ruddy-faced captain gave Sammi a wink.
"How are you enjoying your ride?"

She grinned. "It's beautiful, but I'm a little cold. You
said I could come in here, right?"

He nodded. "You've got a fancy camera there, missy.
With the way you was snappin' pictures out there, I'd take
you for a professional. But ya' look mighty young to be one
if you don't mind me saying so." The captain's face seemed
to get redder the more he spoke.

Sammi tried not to laugh. "I *am* a professional photographer."

His small blue eyes searched hers, waiting for more information. Sammi bit her lip. She could see this was something he wasn't about to let go. "What is it about me that
everyone has to know how I could possibly be a professional photographer?"

"Ya don't look old enough."

At that comment Sammi took a seat next to the captain,
who was standing at the helm. "I got a scholarship to the
Brooks Institute in California, where I majored in photography. Have you heard of it?"

"Nope."

"It's a school for the arts. During my senior year of college, *Global Explorer* magazine offered me one of their
coveted internships. They liked my work so much, they offered me a job when I graduated."

"Sounds like you're a lucky lady."

"Sometimes," she mused.

For the next half hour they sat in silence. There was

nothing in the world Sammi hated more than silence. She needed to be doing something—anything—but this just had to end!

"I was wondering. How many types of bears and birds are on the island? Oh, and what species of flowers and trees are indigenous? And then—"

"Hold on now, little missy. That's a lot of questions for a sea captain." He pointed to the U.S. Forest Service truck. She got up from her seat to get a good look at the beaten-up vehicle loaded on the ferry.

"That's Chief Powell inside, the head ranger up here in the Tongass National Forest. He can answer all your questions. He's a good man. You can trust him. Just warn him first that you're there to interview him, not for small talk."

A smile spread across Sammi's face. "Thank you." She reached over and kissed the captain's cheek. After looking at her watch, she saw she had exactly an hour and a half to pick the chief's brain.

Sammi reached for her camera case, purse and backpack before heading out the door into the strong wind. She threw her backpack in the truck bed and knocked on the driver's window.

As it rolled down, a vicious wind whipped up Sammi's hair from all directions, causing her to lose every bit of professionalism.

"Young lady?" a strong male voice called out. "You'll need to remove your bag from the truck."

"What? I can't hear you! The wind!"

Embarrassed, considering this was their initial meeting, Sammi reached in her pocket and found an elastic. She used it to tie her hair back in a ponytail, letting her wispy bangs flow where they might.

"Hi," she said. Her eyes finally met his. As she looked at the dark, attractive ranger, she felt her usually fearless attitude slip away.

When the captain had said "Chief Powell," she'd thought of Yogi Bear, Grizzly Adams—not some green-eyed hottie with rugged features and dark curly hair. Wow! She hoped he hadn't seen her blush.

"Have we met before?"

"No." Why would he say that?

"Hmm… You need to remove your bag from my truck immediately. This is a government vehicle, not tourist transportation."

When she gave him no response, his mood changed from anger to annoyance. "Are you okay? Do you need some seasickness pills?"

Pull yourself together, Sammi.

Everyone who knew her would be laughing at her. She was checking out a guy in a park ranger uniform. Ohh, she was losing her mind.

The ranger moved fast, lowering himself from the truck in mere seconds. He was taller than she'd anticipated. It forced her to tilt her head back to look at him.

"Let's check your vitals," he muttered, grasping her wrist. Here was the first guy who'd knocked her socks off and he thought she was an irritating, seasick tourist!

He was looking at her again. "Your pulse is a little high, but nothing to worry about."

My heart is racing!

He bent down to examine Sammi a little closer. "You don't look green. Your pupils aren't dilated. Would you mind telling me what's going on?"

Sammi knew she needed to act fast to diffuse this situation. "I'm sorry for this horrible introduction. I'm Samantha Danbury." She put on her most charming smile and held out her hand.

Chief Powell leaned back against his truck and slipped on his sunglasses before shaking it. "Listen, Samantha. You seem like a nice girl, but I'm just not interested in dating anyone right now. Go tell Captain Lovell to stop trying to set me up." He started to open the door to his cab.

Now she knew why Captain Lovell had told her to ask quickly for the interview. *The man's an egomaniac.*

Samantha's blood began to boil. "Listen here, Chief Powell," she said. "I have no idea what you're talking about. Like I said before, I'm Samantha Danbury with *Global Explorer* magazine."

She fumbled in her purse and pulled out her journalist ID. "I'm a freelance photographer for the magazine and I'm here to do a piece on the fisherman of Craig, Alaska. A man by the name of Nels Engstrom is going to be helping me with it."

Good lie, Sammi. Hope it's true.

"Nels? Nels Engstrom? The crusty old salt?" The chief stood up, looking shocked. "The man barely talks," he muttered.

Sammi mustered every bit of control to hide her joy. Her grandpa was alive! "Just the same," she interjected, "I was asking Captain Lovell about some of the flora and fauna on the island, and he said you'd be a good person to talk to. But I can see you're definitely not the guy."

She began to walk to the rear of the truck, reaching in for her backpack. Suddenly she felt the chief's warm body in back of her. The fact that she was affected by such close proximity let her know that she needed to get a life. It had been a long time since she'd been on a date. Hanging out with reporters and cameramen didn't count.

"Um, I'm not the best at apologies," he said. "We're a

close-knit community up here. It seems I'm always getting set up. It was rude of me to assume that's what was going on, but when you didn't say anything and you weren't sick, I didn't know what else to think."

She felt him clasp her hand and lead her to the other side of the cab. He opened the door to help her get in. The truck was cool, but got instantly warmer when the chief climbed in the driver's side again.

He's obviously a jerk. Ask your questions, be professional and try not to think that he's the first man you've been attracted to in months.

With her little pep talk done, Sammi felt ready to take on Chief Powell. He started the engine to heat the cab. As soon as that was done, he focused his full attention on her.

"You can call me Jake. Everyone else does." His smile put her at ease. "So what do you want to know, Samantha?"

For once her name sounded so young. "Just call me Sam."

"All right, Sam, ask away. Just no pictures of me, all right?"

She nodded. "Deal."

The next hour or so flew by. Though she gathered a lot of information in that amount of time, Sammi felt she'd barely skimmed the surface of this paradise. Too soon the ferry reached shore and the cars drove onto an island covered with a beautiful, lush, green rain forest.

As the truck made its way onto the gangplank, Sammi turned around in her seat to look at the ferry. "Oh—I need to go back and thank Captain Lovell."

"Don't worry. I'll tell him for you," Jake offered.

"Promise?"

"Yep."

"Thanks. He was so nice to help me get a trip over here. I had no idea how crowded this place would be this time of year."

"So is that what you do? Just fly around the world to wherever your next idea takes you?" Jake eyed her curiously as if searching her soul.

"No," she answered after a thoughtful pause. "Mostly I go where the magazine tells me. This is the first time I've been able to pick a location."

"Why Alaska?"

"Why not?"

"I don't know. You don't look like a woman who would come to Alaska."

"What does that mean? What kind of women come here?"

"Old women."

"Old women?"

"You know. The kind who take retirement cruises."

Sammi sat back in her seat and laughed harder than she had in ages. "Good one, Jake. Sometimes people surprise you."

"You've been an interesting surprise today, Sam."

"Hopefully not too horrible."

"Quite the opposite. I enjoy discussing my home. I hope you got the information you needed."

"Yes and no. There's a running joke at the magazine that I overresearch." She thought of the many pranks that had been done at her expense.

"So you like your job?"

"Getting paid to travel and take pictures is every photographer's dream."

"You like excitement?"

Images of the tsunami began to flood her mind. She closed her eyes and took a deep breath. "It depends."

Jake must have sensed she didn't want to discuss this anymore. "Where should I take you?" he asked her.

"Drop me off at the rental shop right over there."

Quicker than she wanted, he had her luggage at the door of the store. He opened her side of the truck.

"Thanks for your help."

"You're welcome, Sam. I'm sure I'll see you around at the Fourth of July festivities."

"Really?"

"Really. I live near Nels and we all tend to run into each other from time to time." Jake gave her a devilish smile, swung back into the truck and drove away.

Chapter Two

Two hours later, Sammi still hadn't found transportation to Craig. All flights, cars, buses and charters were booked for the next two days. It was the same story everywhere. "It's the Fourth of July, Miss. All amenities are booked unless you're willing to pay high premiums."

Money! The cursed thing she never had. Before she'd left the Maldives, the magazine had finally wired her the amount of money she'd lost in the tsunami. Between paying back Max de Roussillac, her mother's new husband, and booking a flight to Alaska, she would have to be careful till she got paid again. Who knew when that would be?

Sammi hated hitchhiking, but it seemed that would be her only way to cross the thirty-one-mile-wide island. She'd hitchhiked through Europe and parts of Asia, always carrying Mace for protection. Hopefully, she could find a nice family on vacation driving by who would be willing to help a stranded female.

Hefting her heavy backpack, she headed to the highway and started walking along the shoulder while she waited for a car. What an incredible world! It felt like a wild wonderland where the second you stepped off the road you could get swallowed up in nature. There were lakes and streams hidden behind trees, with eagles flying around as if it was an everyday occurrence. Of course it was normal *here,* but not to her.

Towering hemlocks, spruces and western cedars surrounded her. The rain forest floor was alive and green. Birds soared and little mouselike creatures—the voles Jake had told her about?—dived into their burrows when they heard her footsteps. It was beyond beautiful.

Suddenly a black-tailed doe came into view with her fawn, pausing to take a drink at a small creek. Sammi lowered her things to the ground. After she got out her camera, she began snapping shots of the family.

While she was taking pictures, she heard an old truck roaring down the highway. The sound reminded her of the loud V-8 engine trucks that would come to the vineyard bringing hired help, especially at harvest time. When it rolled to a stop behind her, her adrenaline began to kick in. The deer pranced away at the intrusion, and Sammi reached for the Mace tucked into her jeans.

"Take it you didn't call ahead of time even to book a scooter." The chief ranger!

Relief, exhilaration and excitement filled her all at once. She turned around and looked at her rescuer. He was so handsome. She couldn't believe how attracted she was to this life-size Boy Scout.

"A scooter?" Sammi was trying to picture herself on one. She'd probably tip over. In the end she couldn't stop one corner of her mouth from lifting.

"Is that a smile I see?" His voice was full of mirth. "For such a world traveler, you seem to be very unprepared for this interview."

Sammi stood up and began walking toward him at a brisk pace. "You're not catching me at my best!" She hated not looking professional. Hopefully, he wouldn't figure out her true agenda before she'd met her grandparents.

Jake shook his head. "Temper, temper."

AS SAM DREW CLOSER Jake raked a hand through his hair, feeling more dirt. All the while he cursed himself for not having taken a shower back at the station in Hollis. This woman was a fun diversion from his regular duties in the park. At the moment he didn't know if that was good or bad, but he didn't really care.

Though a professional photographer, Sam could easily be in front of the camera herself. She had to be one of the most beautiful women he'd ever seen. Talk about irresistible, with silky blond hair hanging halfway down her back and a fringe of bangs framing her angelic face.

Those eyes… The intense, deep sapphire-blue drew him in. He definitely wanted to get to know this sassy little thing better.

And that walk. She was going to stop traffic in Craig, especially in those hip-hugging jeans. Now that they were just a foot apart, he realized she barely came to his shoulders. Though she was tiny, she had curves in all the right places. He lowered his head to look down at her, waiting for her to say something.

"What are you doing out here, Chief?"

Jake took a relaxed stance and folded his arms. "I was driving when I noticed some gear on the side of the road. Typically a bad sign." He pretended to shiver at the possibilities. His voice quieted. "There are bears out here, you know."

"I'm aware of that. We discussed it on the ferry. You told me they tend to stay clear of busy places."

"True, but I thought I'd check out the situation, anyway.

As chief ranger, I'm sworn to protect women stranded on the side of the road."

Sammi shook her head. "Is that in the oath you take?"

"The real question is, why didn't you tell me you didn't have a ride?"

"I just figured there had to be some type of transportation." She held up her palm. "Stop. I know. I've heard it a hundred times today—it's the height of the tourist season. But I've hitchhiked all over the world and I've been fine."

"You're a crazy woman, Sam Danbury."

"You have to be, in my business."

Jake let out a sigh. "I'll take you to Craig. All you had to do was ask." He walked to his truck and put her bag in the back. "Climb in. The door's open."

"Thank you." Sammi reached in her purse and pulled out more than enough money to cover gas expenses.

"What's that for?" Jake eyed the cash warily.

"Gas money?"

He shook his head going around to the driver's side. "Up here it's an insult to pay people for hospitality. Besides, I was headed in that direction anyway."

Sammi climbed in, relieved she was on her way. After a minute she said, "How do you ever get used to this beauty?"

"I hope I never do. I grew up here. The older I've gotten, the more I've learned to appreciate it."

"What a childhood you must have had," she said in a soft voice.

"A boy's dream." He took a calming breath, still having a hard time getting over the picture of Sam alone on the side of the road. For some reason he already felt protective of her. It had to be the ranger in him.

"Jake…" Her voice broke through his thought processes. "Jake?"

"What?"

"Can this truck *handle* ninety miles an hour? We're going pretty fast." Sam looked worried, but her smile was dangerous. She was the kind of girl who could get to a guy.

He patted the steering wheel. "This baby may be old, but she can take it."

"All right then." His passenger leaned back and looked out the window, taking in the scenery.

"Speaking of luck, do you always get in the car of anyone who will pick you up?"

"No. Just big Boy Scouts like you."

"We rangers have our dark sides." His voice had dropped an octave.

Sammi's heart began to pound. "What do you mean?"

"We might tell someone a hike isn't that hard. To us it isn't, but…"

Sammi started laughing. "But you have to go out and find them once they're lost on some rugged trail, right?"

"Yeah. But it's a good way to introduce tourists to the real Alaska."

She couldn't stop staring at his chiseled face, emphasized by his dark coloring and lazy smile. "You're horrible."

"Absolutely, and once in a while I might get to help out a good-looking stranded woman."

At that comment Sammi could see there was more to this ranger than met the eye. Men didn't really fit into her life or her job, not to mention the fact that she was here to find her grandparents. Jake could definitely complicate her time up here.

He relaxed back in the seat as he drove. It was time for Sammi to change the subject. "Tell me—how is it that you know the Engstroms?"

"My dad and their deceased son, Chris, were best friends growing up."

The revelation startled Sammi. In her research she'd discovered that Craig was a small town. Most of the people on the island knew each other, but what were the odds of her meeting the son of her father's best friend?

She'd never been one to look for signs or believe in fate, but maybe for once her father was looking out for her. Was it possible?

You're going crazy, Sammi.

In the pictures she'd found in the journal, Jake's father must have been the boy standing next to her dad.

"Sam? Have you heard a word I've said?"

"What?"

Jake eyed her curiously. "Are you okay?"

"I'm tired. I just flew in from the Maldives."

"They just had that tsunami." He sounded concerned.

"I know. I lived through it and photographed the destruction. Very sad." Sammi reached up to rub her eyes.

"How are you dealing with all of that?" he asked in a low tone.

"Me? I'm fine," she lied. It haunted her day and night. Between her mother's deception about the existence of her grandparents, and now the tsunami, she didn't think she could ever be whole again. "Please forgive my rudeness. I guess I'm more exhausted than I realized. Tell me what you were saying."

"Since my dad is one of the Engstroms' only connections to Chris, our family has spent a lot of time with them. We—I—have a brother who lives in San Francisco," Jake added. "We became the Engstroms' adopted grandchildren. That's why I'm so surprised that Nels would let anyone near him now."

His revelation sent a shudder through her body. "What do you mean, he doesn't let anyone near him?"

"Ever since his son died tragically, he's never been the same. He doesn't like to talk to strangers."

"How sad. I've lost loved ones, too. It can be very painful." Sammi was silent for a moment. "So you have a brother in San Francisco. I'm from California. St. Helena, not San Fran. I grew up on a vineyard. My mom's an artist and we lived a very simple life in the country. I prefer towns to cities."

It was so hard to think her grandfather was still suffering after all these years. What if the knowledge of Sammi's existence could have helped? Why had her mom assumed keeping everything a secret had been the right thing to do?

Lost in thought, Sammi didn't realize the truck had come to a stop. "What's wrong?"

"Black bears."

Sammi stared out the front window at the large, furry animals. She longed to get out her camera and capture the magnificent creatures in their natural habitat. But for some reason she couldn't move just yet. "What do you do in these situations?"

He leaned closer to her. "Feed them." His voice had gone real quiet.

"What kind of food?"

"Tourists."

She blinked. "You!"

Her companion smiled and winked at her. Sammi looked around the cab for something to throw at him. It seemed an empty bag that had held jerky was all she could find. She tossed it at him, making him laugh.

He caught it and said, "A bag of jerky would bring a black bear after you faster than you could scream for help."

Quicker then a flash, he reached in back of him and grabbed a rifle. Rolling down the window, he shot off two rounds. The sound sent the bears scurrying into the woods.

"See—bears sometimes are on the road. That's why I don't leave women walking along the shoulder, snapping pictures."

Sammi felt like a fool. "Next time I do a trip like this again, I'll make certain I'm better prepared."

Jake started up the truck again and continued their drive along the scenic route. She turned to look out the window once more. After a few minutes she got a little nerve back and glanced at his strong profile. Oh, boy, she was in trouble!

He was simply too attractive. It felt natural to be sitting with him, listening to old rock songs as he maneuvered the truck through this paradise. It was comforting to be looked after for once, even if only for a couple of hours. What would it be like to have a man like Jake in her life? But those were dreams she didn't dare entertain. Her job didn't allow her to have romantic relationships.

Focus! You're here to learn about your dad and meet your grandparents. Not to become involved with Ranger Rick.

To get her mind off her feelings, Sammi decided to continue interviewing him. He seemed amenable. For the rest of the trip she learned that he conducted studies on the indigenous fish of Alaska for the National Forest Service, be they in streams and lakes or in the Southwest Passage.

The time flew by. Before long they drew near to Craig. Sammi could see the small islands connected by causeways that made up the small fishing town. From what she'd learned, Nels lived just outside of the community.

Jake pulled onto a gravel road heading around a cove. Three homes loomed ahead. Two were built on stilts near the sea; the other was higher up the green mountain.

His truck came to a stop at the first one. "Here we are." The white clapboard house was charming in a run-down kind of way. "There's Nels's old fishing boat moored at the dock. Looks like he's waiting to give you that interview."

She followed Jake out of the truck and walked up the flight of stairs, where he rang the doorbell. Her heart was pounding wildly.

An older couple answered the door. They were the people from the pictures in her dad's journal, and they seemed excited to see Jake.

Sammi experienced a thrill to discover that both her grandparents were alive. She'd read everything her dad had written about her grandma Marta and grandfather Nels many times. She couldn't believe this moment had finally come.

Her grandma spoke first. "Who's this, Jake?"

Before he could answer, Sammi said, "I'm your granddaughter, Samantha Danbury."

Chapter Three

Sammi's declaration might as well have set off an explosion. Both Jake and Marta started flinging questions at her so fast she couldn't have answered them if she'd wanted to.

As the situation escalated, her gaze remained fixed on a pair of blue eyes that looked just like hers. Nels Engstrom didn't say a word, but the look of acceptance on his face astounded her.

He was a fit man with gray hair who looked to be in his mid-seventies. His face, weathered from his years at sea, wore a smile that would put a child at ease. Sammi judged him to be around five foot nine or so, but it was hard to tell, especially when he stood next to Jake, who seemed larger than life in every way.

Her grandfather stepped away from the others and reached out to her. Sammi could feel a lump in her throat, and blinked. "Would you like proof who I am? I have a birth certificate and pictures with me."

When Jake and Marta saw what was happening to her, they both stopped their questions. Sammi could feel all eyes on her. She'd found her dad's family. This was the moment she'd dreamed of all her life.

Nels's smile got bigger. His eyes began to swim in tears.

"I don't need a birth certificate to know my own granddaughter. You're the spitting image of your father when he left us."

Sammi's whole body trembled. She couldn't stop the flood of her own tears. He *knew* she was his granddaughter!

"Samantha? Can you come and give your grandpa a hug? That's what all our other grandkids call me."

She walked slowly into Nels's arms and sobbed on his shoulder. If her father hadn't died, she sensed this was what it would have been like to be loved by him. Yet along with her joy, she felt anger over missing out on twenty-three years of knowing her grandparents.

Obviously not one to be ignored, her grandmother got in on the moment. She was petite, like Sammi, in both height and stature. Marta had pretty features and silver-blond hair, pulled back in a bun. She wore a colorful apron over her clothes.

She grabbed Sammi's shoulders and looked her square in the eye. The inspection became more intense as her hands moved to Sam's face. "You look like my Chris in your eyes and in bone structure, but when you smile you're a knockout, dear. Who's your mother? How come we didn't know about you before now? Did our Chris know he had a daughter?"

Her questions sounded so sincere, her voice so emotional. Marta was hurting as much as Sammi. Tears misted her grandmother's green-flecked eyes.

Mom, you're the reason for this.

This was going to be so much harder than Sammi had thought. How did you tell people your mother had lied to you all your life? The woman you'd loved, who'd raised you. The woman you'd trusted beyond all else…

Sammi fought a new onslaught of tears by digging her fingernails into her palms until they hurt. "It's a long story."

At that Jake started laughing. "A long story. That's all you have to say?"

The threesome could see the humor of the situation and smiles shone through tearstained faces.

Marta collected herself first. "Jake? You're filthy, son. You need a shower." She gave him a no-nonsense look. "When are you ever going to learn to take one before you come home from trips?"

"I'm aware of that, Marta, but you're not getting rid of me so easily. I'm going to stay to hear this story."

"All right." Marta squeezed Sammi's shoulder. "Let's go inside and hear this before I go insane with questions." She guided her into the charming home.

NELS HEADED DOWN TO THE truck to collect Sammi's things.

Jake followed. "Nels? How are you so sure this woman is your granddaughter? It could be a trick. I'd be happy to run some background checks. I don't want you or Marta to be hurt."

The older man stopped once he reached the truck, putting both hands on the side of the cab for support. "You've never had a child, Jake. Since my Chris died, there's not a night that goes by I don't wake, thinking of him."

He reached in to pull out Sammi's bag. "When that girl stood on my doorstep just moments ago, I thought it was a ghost. She looks like an Engstrom. One day when you have kids and grandkids you'll understand." He patted Jake on the arm, then carried everything inside the house.

"I don't have that ability to trust. Family can let you down. I learned that from C.J.," Jake muttered to himself before getting in his truck to make a quick phone call. Five minutes later he hung up.

Tomorrow I'll find out if this girl is for real or not.

Just as he was getting back out again, he saw another truck, heading from his parents' home to the Engstroms'. He slammed the door shut. "Of course they called Mom and Dad."

Sam was going to drive him crazy and he'd only known her five hours.

Jake leaned against his truck. A little later he waved to his family. It must have taken Marta all of two minutes to track them down. By now half of Craig would know about Sam. In another hour the rest would know, too. It was one of the few drawbacks of living in a small town.

The big black Chevy truck pulled into the circular driveway, kicking up dust as it came to a stop. Jake nodded to his father before heading to the other door to help his mom out.

Doug Powell levered himself from the cab with ease and headed around the vehicle. He took Jake by the arm before he could open the door. "Is it really true you found Chris's daughter by accident and brought her home?"

The hope Jake saw in his father's eyes was unbelievable. His dad was a quiet fisherman who worked hard to put food on the table. According to Jake's grandmother, Doug had been a lighthearted soul before Jake was born, but his carefree spirit had died when news of Chris's accident came.

"I don't know, Dad. She has a birth certificate and some pictures. I'm doing a background check on her right now. I won't know for sure until tomorrow."

"But what do you think?"

Images of Sam filled his mind with thoughts he didn't want to share with anyone. He already felt protective of her. Though he didn't like her deception, he understood her motives in wanting to meet Nels and Marta first, before telling people she was Chris Engstrom's long-lost daughter. It seemed like a fairy tale that could come crashing down and hurt the whole family. He'd feel better once he made sure she was for real. Hell, he *still* wanted to get to know her better.

"It would be an amazing blessing for Marta and Nels if she really is Chris's daughter."

Doug reached out and gave him a bear hug, something he hadn't done in years. "You always were my cautious one, Jakey."

Jakey? What was going on? His whole family was going crazy.

Doug's voice dropped to a whisper. "It's an unforeseen gift from God in Nels's older years. Maybe now he'll finally be able to forgive himself."

Jake put an arm on his dad's shoulder. "Now that *would* be a miracle."

His father gave him another giant hug. "Let's get your mom inside." He let go of him and opened the door for Doris Powell, Jake's tall, thin, dark-haired mother. She wasn't a beauty in the regular sense, but she had strength and a great sense of humor. These qualities had gotten their family through the good times and the bad.

"Sounds like you brought home a real catch for once, Jake!" She gave him a hug and a sly wink. No doubt they would all fall for Sam's charms, too.

As his father led her up the porch steps, she called over her shoulder, "Your brother is following us in your new Jeep, with Beastly. He's been having a blast wheeling it around the island."

"Ah, mom. Where did he find the keys?"

"I tried to stop him, honey."

Sure she did. Like a baby stops someone trying to take its candy, his mother could never refuse C.J. anything. But before Jake could say a word, his parents had disappeared inside the house.

He could hear the Jeep, but he couldn't see it. The way his brother was driving, he'd break his new custom speakers and wheel kit. Instead of waiting in the driveway, Jake took off at a clip, running up the emerald-forested hill behind the house. He knew where C.J. had gone.

There was an old logging road hidden in the trees. When they were young they always used it as a shortcut to the Engstroms' house. Once Jake reached the top of the hill he saw his brand-new, four-door Wrangler wheeling up the steep incline. C.J. had taken the top off. The dog sat in the passenger seat, loving life.

Beastly, you traitor!

It was payback time. Jake stood on a rock behind a tree so his brother wouldn't see him before he jumped in the Jeep to scare him.

MARTA AND NELS TOOK SAMMI on a short tour of their home, pointing out pictures of her father as a child. The cozy place had knickknacks everywhere, a wide-open floor plan and a great room surrounding a fireplace that emanated warmth. To her friends back at Brooks—a university for the arts—this place would be a makeover dream. But to Sammi it was perfect! Exactly how a grandparent's house should look.

Nels reached for her bags and led her up the rickety old staircase to the upper level, which was painted a cheery yellow. The home was bigger than it appeared. To her surprise she learned there were three bedrooms and two bathrooms.

Marta followed closely behind, pointing out the bathroom Sammi could use to freshen up in. They set her up in her father's old room, the one she was told he'd shared with one of his two older brothers.

"I'll put some tea on, dear. Come down when you're

ready." Her grandmother squeezed her hand and walked away. Nels gave Sammi a gentle nod before trailing his wife out the door.

Once it was shut, Sammi sat on one of the twin beds and looked around the room. It was full of trophies and pictures. There was so much life to learn about and so much pain to overcome....

She leaned back on the bed and closed her eyes. The memory of Nels and his loving embrace kept coming back to her, assuring her this was real—this was really happening!

Sammi knew they were dying for answers, but freshening up sounded like heaven. After coming from the hot weather of the tropics to the Alaskan summer, she was chilled to the bone. The ferry ride over had been cold, and then meeting Jake...

Jake! Because she hadn't told him the whole truth, she wondered what he thought of her now. Hopefully, he would understand.

Sammi felt exhausted and knew a hot shower would do the trick. A half hour later she emerged from the bathroom ready to take on the world. She put on some comfy jeans tucked into fuzzy boots, and topped off her look with a pink cowl-neck sweater.

She decided to wear her long hair down and minimal makeup. After retrieving her father's journal from her backpack, she was ready to tell her grandparents the whole story.

Once she left the bedroom she could hear a rumble of voices in the great room below. What was going on? Who was here?

As she made her way down the stairs her hands shook. At the landing she stopped, finding a group of people staring up at her.

"For once you actually caught something worth bringing home!"

"Shut it, Jeremiah!"

Two of the most handsome men she'd ever seen came forward to meet her on the stairs. They looked alike, but all she noticed was her ranger, with eyes as green as the island he lived on. Even if he'd stayed at the house for no other reason than to hear her story, maybe he'd stick around after? A girl could hope.

She let out a nervous laugh. "You're a twin! I can only imagine the damage you two boys did growing up here in Craig." Her eyes never left Jake's. She couldn't help but notice how incredible he looked up close. He was still in his ranger outfit and needed a shower, but there was something so irresistible about this guy.

Jake was suddenly shoved aside and another Jake stood in front of her, perfectly groomed. This guy was a charmer and knew it!

"Hi, Samantha. I'm Christopher Powell, but everyone calls me C.J. Only Jacob here calls me Jeremiah." He held out his hand to shake hers politely. "Sorry you had to meet the brute of the family." Jake's twin gave her a sexy smile and a wink. His eyes were the same shade of green as Jake's. C.J. was obviously comfortable using his looks to his advantage. Sammi might have fallen for his charms if she hadn't met the Boy Scout first.

"Hi." She felt uncomfortable under C.J.'s gaze and looked around anxiously for Jake, who'd gone over to sit in a lounge chair by the fireplace. His green eyes were still focused on her. They looked just as playful as they'd been when he'd found her at the side of the road this afternoon.

"Told you, Jeremiah," he teased his brother. "Sam isn't fooled by charm and idiocy."

Sammi's attention was caught by a large dog warming himself at Jake's feet. "That's funny," she murmured. "I don't think I noticed a dog before."

"This is Beastly, the love of my life." At the mention of her name, the dog raised her head.

"Jake?" She eyed him intently. "Who are all these people?"

"Well, besides your grandparents, that's my brother, as you can see. The two people on the couch are my parents, Doris and Doug Powell."

"Oh!" She smiled shyly. "It's a pleasure to meet all of you."

They smiled in response and then waited for her to sit. Sammi pulled herself together and walked over to where Nels sat on the sofa. Once seated, she could see the Pacific Ocean out the window. "What a view!"

"You like it, dear?" Marta had just come from the kitchen.

"I love it!"

"I'm glad. But, Samantha—do you think you could start to explain? I'm not sure we can wait much longer." She sat on the other side of the couch, next to Sammi, and patted her hand. "Since Doug and Chris were best friends growing up, we invited him and his family over. I called our two other boys—your dad's brothers—but they live in Seattle and Anchorage, and won't be able to get here for a couple of days."

Sammi noticed C.J. had taken his place on a lounge chair next to his parents. Jake stayed by the fireplace. He obviously liked to keep aloof. She wished he was next to her instead of over there with his dog.

Taking a quick breath, she began her story, explaining the reasons why her mother had kept everything a secret. Sammi told them about her childhood on the vineyard in St. Helena with her mom and Aunty Edna. She talked about the owner of the vineyard, Steve de Roussillac, his kindness, and how he'd helped her mom raise Sammi.

She spoke of the beauty of the landscape and how it had prompted her to start taking photographs. Finally she explained how her mom had just married Max de Roussillac, Steve's son, and how hurt Sammi was that her mom had kept her grandparents' identity hidden.

Sammi then turned her attention to Nels, who'd been listening attentively. "I'm curious. Why did my dad leave Alaska? What was he paying you back for? Why do you think he wouldn't have told you about us?"

Nels promptly got up and walked to the fireplace. Sammi realized she had overstepped her boundaries, and felt the blood drain from her face.

Marta clasped Sammi's chin. "Your father and Nels didn't part on the best of terms." Her voice had grown quiet.

Nels turned toward her, looking at Sam through anguished eyes. "My Chris was a troublemaker. I was too hard on him."

"Nels—you were only doing what any father would do," Doug interjected.

"No!" His voice shook with pain. "I drove my Chris away. One night he took my fishing boat out while he was drunk and crashed it. I was furious. The things I said hurt him to the point that he felt he could never come home until he'd repaid me.

"I wanted him to come to his senses. Tragically, it wasn't until his death that I came to mine. Every day since then I've had to live with the pain of losing my son. Bless the Lord for sending you to our home, Samantha. You're welcome here for as long as you want to be with us." On that note, Nels went upstairs.

Why did you keep everything a secret, Mom?

It was dark by the time the Powells went home. Two o'clock in the morning rolled around before Sammi climbed into bed. There'd been tears, laughter, but mostly feelings of loss.

Her very last thought was of Jake and how he'd said goodbye to her. Had he meant it to be a final goodbye, or only until tomorrow?

Chapter Four

Sammi woke up the next morning more tired than ever. Her dreams had been vivid and often turned dark. She couldn't quite remember what she dreamed of, but the demons that had haunted her over the last months were obviously surfacing.

To her chagrin she hadn't been able to warm up, and she hoped she would acclimatize soon. Normally, it never took this long.

I must still be in shock.

As if the cold wasn't enough, she felt her heart was being torn in two. While she was thrilled to be with her grandparents, she knew her mom was worried about her.

I know I need to call you, Mom, and tell you what I learned about Dad. I just can't do it yet. Maybe I'll send an e-mail after breakfast.

Sammi left her bed and went to the window. The view staggered her, and instantly a change came over her as she took in the magic of her surroundings. A layer of mist clung to the calm waters of the steel-blue sea. Above it, tiny rays of sunshine broke through the cloud cover, bringing the mist to life with colors of yellow and peach.

The cove where her grandparents lived looked out on small islands covered in lush green forests, typical of the magnificent ocean vistas around Prince of Wales Island. Sammi walked to another window, noting there was so much to do. From the moment you stepped off the front porch, it was a hiker's dream. Rocky shores led up to the forest, where fallen trees were sure to be home to small animals and a host of interesting fungi. The deeper her gaze penetrated the woods, the more intense was the foliage. She could only imagine the treasures waiting to be found.

I bet Jake knows some amazing places.

The idea of being alone with him set off her adrenaline. Would he want to spend time with her?

This was where her father had grown up. Sammi couldn't wait to get out and snap pictures. How could she ever take enough photos of such a place? The wildlife, the plants, the landscape—all of it was a photographer's dream.

She hurried and got dressed in jeans, hiking boots and a white turtleneck, ready to take on the day. Not wanting to deal with her hair, she pulled it back into a long braid, letting her bangs sweep softly to the side. Once she learned what her grandparents had planned for the day, she hoped she could fit in a hike for a couple of hours.

As she entered the great room, the smell of a hot breakfast wafted past her nose. She spotted Nels eating at the table while he read the newspaper. "Good morning," she called out.

"You're up early, dear." Marta poked her head out from behind the refrigerator door.

"Is it early?"

"Seven-thirty." Nels spoke from behind his paper.

"Oh."

"What do you like for breakfast?" her grandmother asked.

"I usually have coffee and some toast, but I can get it myself."

"Oh, no, you don't. This is my kitchen and I'm the captain."

While Marta was talking, Nels put the paper down and smiled at Sammi. He motioned for her to take a seat at the large, oval wooden table. "There's no use in fighting her. Our daughters-in-law gave up years ago," he whispered.

Sammi smiled back. "Okay." It was fun to have little family secrets like this. *Family.* It was going to take some getting used to.

Marta brought the food over—a spread of eggs, bacon, coffee, juice and toast. Sammi found herself eating and drinking more than she normally did this early in the morning. It had been too long since she'd had such a delicious, home-cooked breakfast.

They chatted while enjoying the morning. There were more questions about what Sammi did for a living, where she'd traveled in and out of America, where she'd gone to school and what made her fall in love with photography.

"I would have to say Mom got me into it. I was given a Polaroid camera for my sixth birthday and went around the vineyard snapping pictures. My mom thought they were wonderful and used them as models for her own artwork. She painted a whole series of tiles that sold for a lot of money that year."

Nels pushed his plate away and looked at her a little more seriously than he had before. "Samantha, I talked to your mom on the phone this morning."

A wave of emotion almost crippled her. She didn't know exactly how to react. How did you get mad at someone you didn't know that well? Sammi could understand his reasons, but she felt betrayed. "How did you find her number?"

"You left the journal down here. I saw a business card with your mom's name on it. So I called."

"All right."

"Your mama is awful worried about you. There were times when we hadn't heard from our Chris for what felt like ages. As parents we make mistakes, but that doesn't stop us from worrying or loving."

Last night Nels had stood at the fireplace a broken man. Sammi knew he'd phoned her mother because he'd thought it was right. She drummed her fingers on the table, trying to control her turbulent emotions.

"How can you forgive her so easily for keeping this secret for twenty-three years?"

Nels put his hand on Sammi's. "We lost our boy." His voice cracked. "Life is too precious to waste on the past. I've been trying to move forward for twenty-three years, but I didn't know if that was possible until I saw you on the front porch yesterday. That's what I told your mom.

"I believe it's a miracle that you're here. I thanked her for raising an amazing daughter and taking such good care of her. Your dad would be proud. I know *we* are."

Sammi got up and hugged him. "Thank you." She moved on to hug Marta. "I don't know when I'll be able to forgive her."

"Time, dear. Just give yourself some time," her grandmother said as she gently rubbed Sammi's hair.

She took her seat again. "I was thinking I might rent a room in town for when I'm not working. For the next little while I would like to get to know you two better. What do you think?" She bit her lip, waiting anxiously for their response.

Nels stood up and took his plate to the kitchen sink. "I think that's a fine plan, except no grandchild of mine sleeps anywhere but in our home." His voice had turned firm, but the vulnerability in his eyes was still evident. She was comforted to know he wanted her there with them.

The noise of an engine caught their attention. Nels looked out the window and started laughing. "It looks like we might have a little competition, Marta."

"What are you talking about?" his wife asked.

"A certain forest ranger seems to be awfully interested in what's going on over here all of a sudden."

Sammi's stomach filled with butterflies. "Does the forest service come here often?"

Nels shook his head. "Jake hasn't been over here this much since high school. Don't get me wrong—he checks on us from time to time. Just not on a daily basis." Her grandfather's smile was infectious.

The thought of Jake coming to see her sent a jolt of excitement through her. She heard the truck come to a stop, then a knock on the front door. Nels left the kitchen to get it.

Sammi was in a quandary what to do. Should she act excited or wait to see what he wanted? She decided to wait.

NELS OPEN THE DOOR. "Morning, Jake."

"Nels."

"What can I do for you?"

In a quiet voice he said, "I just wanted you to know Samantha's background check cleared. Here's the info." He held out an envelope with the Tongass National Park logo on it.

"Never doubted it."

"You don't want the proof?"

He shook his head. "Already have it. Told you that last night."

"You're a good man, Nels. That's why I'm so protective of you." He folded the envelope and tucked it in his back pocket.

A glimmer shone in Nels's eyes. "Are we finished, son? If so, I'd like to go back to breakfast."

"Wait!" Jake put his hand on the door frame. Automatically, he ran his other hand through his hair. "Once Sam wakes up, would you let her know I'd like to take her to Craig's Annual Third of July show? And Mom wanted me to invite her to the family barbecue tonight."

"Why don't you tell her yourself?"

"She's up?" He could feel his body come alive at the thought of seeing her.

Nels nodded and motioned for him to come inside. Jake couldn't resist. The desire to be with Sam had been the real reason he'd driven over instead of calling. He'd secretly hoped she might be up. Now he was glad he'd come.

They walked through to the kitchen. Sam was a beautiful sight this early. He didn't think he would ever get used to looking at her. "Good morning, Sam."

"Good morning to you." She got out from behind the table to put her dishes in the sink. Her unique little walk was enough to drive a guy mad.

"So what are the Engstroms up to today?"

Marta answered for them all. "We were going to take Sammi to your parents' house for the annual Fourth of July barbecue later. Other than that we thought we'd let her rest after all of her travels."

"Actually, I thought I might take a few pictures of the island," Sammi interjected.

"You can come with me if you'd like," Jake suggested. "I'm heading up to a pretty remote area of the island to check on a research project."

Sammi looked at her grandparents. "Marta? Nels? Is it okay?" She didn't want their feelings to be hurt.

Jake wondered if Sam was naturally this thoughtful.

"Go have a fun time," Marta said with a chuckle.

"That would be great." She hugged her grandma before turning to Jake with a wink. "Maybe I can get your story on the various types of salmon, after all."

He laughed at the comment.

Sammi smiled as she walked past him and headed up the stairs. "Let me get ready. I'll be down in five minutes."

Just now Sam had looked excited, Jake realized. She had a way of getting to him. All he wanted to do was take her away from everyone in his truck and kiss her senseless. Unfortunately, it was the exact sort of activity that would scare her off right now.

Better stick to hiking.

After she'd disappeared, he looked at the Engstroms. "Don't worry. I'll have her back in time for dinner before the fireworks."

"Now listen here, Jacob Powell." Marta had her hands on her hips and a stern expression on her face that Jake hadn't seen since he got caught stealing cookies from her jar when he was a kid. "I'm not too old to see the way you're looking at my granddaughter. You better bring her home early, and no funny business, if you know what I mean."

Nels gave him a knowing eye, seconding her orders. How had Jake gone from adopted grandson to teenage boyfriend predator in just a day?

"Marta, I'm thirty-one and Sam is a woman. We're hardly kids."

"My Sammi—that's what her mamma calls her—is vulnerable, and I won't have you taking advantage of her. You Powell boys have broken enough hearts up here. I won't have you breaking hers." Marta looked like a mother bear ready to strike.

"I'll be on my best behavior."

Sam came down the stairs moments later. The woman clearly had no idea of her appeal to the opposite sex. If she did, she wouldn't be wearing that form-fitting outfit. He didn't know how she could look so attractive in cargo pants and the button-down, anti-bug shirt, but the way they hugged her figure, he realized she had way too much feminine appeal.

Right now he really did feel like a teenager. With Nels and Marta staring warnings at him the whole time he'd been in the house, he'd never felt so unwelcome in his life.

Chapter Five

The trailhead to the Harris River hiking area looked like a secret entrance to a magical world. A midday sun was trying to poke through the frothy clouds, enchanting the forest with dapples of light. Sammi, Jake and Beastly began their walk on the earthen trail, wending their way into this fairyland.

"There aren't as many mosquitoes up here as I've been told."

"We don't have it as bad as they do up north. But it's still no picnic."

"True." She swatted one as she spoke. "Thanks again for the special repellent."

Everywhere she looked the landscape was full of ferns, hemlocks and aspens, with mosses thick at their feet. The trail led them farther into the beauty of this untamed territory. About a quarter mile into their journey Beastly shot ahead into the mist. Sammi figured the dog must have heard something and gone to chase it.

"Will she get lost?"

"Beastly?" Jake's laughter rang out. "That dog knows this island better than I do. She's probably going to the river to see my coworkers."

Sammi nodded. "Out here it feels we're the only people

around." She was having a hard time not staring at Jake and how perfectly he filled out his ranger uniform, with those broad shoulders and long legs. His presence alone would put her at ease here in bear country, even without the gun slung over his back.

"They always have treats for her. She's everyone's favorite girl."

Sammi heard the love Jake had for his dog. "Is she yours?" *What was she thinking, saying that out loud?*

"Absolutely."

"So—does that mean there's no serious girlfriend?"

He kept walking. "When we get up the river aways, I'm going to be busy for a little bit. I need to check the weir—"

"Hey, you didn't answer my question. Is it a touchy subject?" Sammi teased.

She turned around to face Jake, thinking he was a few feet away. Wrong. She was just inches from his tall, muscular body. Sammi tilted her head back to get a good look at him, wishing she were a little taller. At least her hiking boots added a few inches to her five-foot-three frame. She still couldn't believe that a ranger could be so...wow!

Jake pushed his sunglasses on top of his head, then looked down at her and brushed a strand of hair from her cheek. Sammi's knees went weak. He brought both of his hands up to gently caress her face. "There's no girlfriend right now. Does that answer your question?"

"Yes."

The feel of his hands and the tender way he touched her hair made her a little dizzy. Sammi had never been so mentally and physically attracted to a man before. It was shocking.

"What about you? How many boyfriends do you have around the world?" He eyed her lazily.

"Oh, you know, a million or so."

His hands dropped and he took a step back before moving on. "I can believe it."

"Why?" Did he think of her as some man magnet? The love 'em and leave 'em type?

Until now Jake had been very amenable, walking at a pace that allowed Sam the chance to take pictures and ask questions. "Hey! You can't just drop a bomb like that and walk away without an explanation!"

He increased his speed. Sammi found that if she jogged, she was able to keep up with his long strides.

"Tell me!"

"Well," he drawled, "how about the morning we met? You lied about your identity."

"Okay, but that was a first for me. Now that you know the circumstances, you have to understand why."

Jake unexpectedly stopped. When he did, Sammi ran right into him. If he hadn't turned around and steadied her, she would have fallen.

"It's hard to believe anything about you." For the first time since she'd met him, she saw that he'd grown distant. Apparently the playful jokes hid his true feelings.

That *did* hurt. "What are you saying?"

"I'm saying it's hard for a guy like me to understand how you flit around the world, waltzing in and out of people's lives whenever you want, not thinking of those you leave behind."

Her temper was about ready to blow. "That's not fair. You don't know me. I don't flit around the world. I take pictures on locations. The goal of the magazine I work for is to share cultures from around the world with our main readership here in America."

"What about your mom?"

Her jaw clenched tightly.

"Are you going to abandon her the way your father abandoned his parents?" Jake's expression was full of concern. It made everything worse. At least if he were mad she could hate him.

"I can't answer that question right now," she whispered.

"As you can see, Nels has never forgiven himself for what happened with Chris. His death came before anything could be resolved. Don't do that to your mom," Jake urged in a quiet voice.

"This is none of your business," she retorted, and continued up the trail. She wasn't ready to deal with the direction of their conversation. She'd just met her grandparents. Over the last twenty-four hours she'd learned so much. And then there were all the lost years, the lies and the pain of losing trust in your parent.

Mother Nature must have sensed her mood and sent her own tears from the clouds above. Sammi reached in her pack and pulled on her rain slicker, happy for the first time in her life to walk in silence.

She didn't know if she would ever want to talk to Jake Powell again. How dare he tell her how to live her life!

"Sam—stop!" It was a command. What was going on?

Jake came up behind her, cocking his rifle. "Fresh bear tracks," he whispered in her ear.

He pointed his rifle to the side of the trail, pushing Sammi behind him while he looked around. Then he turned to her. "I'm going to check the outer perimeter." He caressed her cheek lightly with his free hand. It sent shivers down her neck. "Stay here. You'll be safe."

She stood in the middle of the once enchanted woods, terrified. Every few seconds she glanced at her watch and waited for Jake's return. The first two minutes crept by. She could hear the forest alive with birds and scurrying animals.

Jake had a way of making her feel so safe. Now every sound, chirp or creak made her jump. Soon the rain abated, but the mist continued to fall. It created shadows that looked like bears coming out of the dense shrubbery. She shivered, yet all she could do was wait. He'd been gone for five minutes now. Where was he?

All of a sudden she could hear a crunching sound coming from the forest. She got the Mace out of her pocket in case it was a bear. A shot of it would give her enough time to run, or take the fetal position before the bear took a swipe at her.

The sound got louder and closer. "Sam, put that down!"

"Jacob Powell!"

"Yes?"

"Don't you ever do that to me again! Next time you go off to find a bear, I'm coming with you. Don't you ever leave me like that! Do you hear me?"

"I hear you, but I had to keep you safe. There was a mama bear with two baby cubs thirty yards away. I needed to make sure they continued in the opposite direction."

"Fine, but take me with you." Sammi's first instinct was to pick up a rock and throw it at him.

"You're a spirited little thing. I figured with all of your travels and boyfriends you'd be used to danger."

"I'm afraid you've lost me again."

"You're an adventurer, like your father. You're living the life he always dreamed of. When my dad heard what you did for a living, he said, 'That's Chris's daughter, all right, and boy, would he be proud.'"

Sammi stepped back and began kicking at the dirt trail under her feet. She took a deep breath before she looked at Jake. "I'm trying to understand something here. How did we go from talking about you not leaving me when bears are around, to my being a heartless wanderer?"

"I've met other photographers like you who come up here, taking pictures for your magazines. You're always looking to have fun. Once you get bored, you're gone."

Sammi contemplated what to do. She still wanted to throw something at him. Or she could run back to the road and hitchhike to Craig, but neither of those ideas would do her any good. She wasn't a coward and she wasn't going to back down from this fight.

He had a warped view of her career. She loved taking pictures. As for a home, she didn't have one. The secret her mom had kept was something Sammi was trying not to think about. And boyfriends weren't even in the picture. It wasn't like she hadn't dated, but her job didn't allow commitments.

"I'm not always looking for a good time, Jake. I go where the magazine sends me. Why would you insinuate I have boyfriends all over the world? Anyway, it's none of your business if I do or don't. I'm only twenty-three. Since when did this conversation turn serious? I like my life. It's a dream come true."

Jake started walking again. The forest grew darker and the mist clung to their bodies the farther they went. This wilderness hike would have been perfect if Jake hadn't ruined it with all his questions.

Fifteen minutes of pure silence passed. To her reckoning, this was the worst quarter hour of her life. Sammi kept looking at her watch, trying to think of something to say.

"So when do you head out on your next adventure?" Jake asked at last.

"He speaks?"

He stopped when they reached a small river. She heard him chuckle. "Do you really hate silence? How do you take good pictures if you can't keep quiet?"

"That's what all the reporters ask. It's the hardest part of the job for me."

Jake's laughter grew louder. It ricocheted around the small clearing they'd just approached. Sammi tried not to smile, but she was extremely self-conscious and had probably turned bright red.

The river looked too deep to cross. She glanced up and down the stream for a log or bridge. That's when the pristine water caught her eye. The ripples were as clear as crystal.

"Do you realize what a paradise you live in?"

"Every day."

Sammi bent and put her hand in the river, letting the cool water flow over her fingers. "Alaska has proved to me that real nature exists in the world, untouched and pure. I've often wondered if I would ever get to see a place like this."

"I'm a completely biased guy, but I don't think anything rivals this place. Admittedly, I haven't traveled much—just to a few conferences in the lower forty-eight. Jeremiah makes fun of me because I've never felt the need to travel. I tell him Alaska is perfection. It's in my blood. It's home."

"Does C.J. hate it when you call him Jeremiah?"

"Oh, yeah."

Sammi loved seeing Jake with such a carefree expression on his face. She stood up and wiped her wet hands on her jeans. She felt more at peace in this setting than at any other time she could remember—as long as the personal questions were at an end for the time being.

"Most of the photos I take for my assignments have to be carefully shot to hide the damage made by human hands. Look around, Jake." She raised her arms and pointed in every direction. "I could take a shot anywhere and not have to hide a thing. Alaska is as pure as nature can get. I'm beginning to think this place may be in my blood more than I realize."

At her words Jake's face turned stoic. She took a deep breath and walked back to the river, listening to the water flowing over the rocks. Sammi felt like a fool for voicing her feelings out loud. She knew better than to do that.

"I forgot to grab waders for you. There's no way to cross this river without getting wet. You can either do that or I can carry you."

Sam liked the last idea. "I really don't want to get wet, so I don't mind if you carry me across."

Jake drew closer.

She flashed him a glance. "Did you do this on purpose, so you would get to carry me?"

He just smiled, leaving her to wonder. Before she knew it, he'd easily picked her up in his arms and started across the river. When Sammi looked at him, his eyes told another story. They were on fire. It sent her pulse racing.

"You never answered my question, Sam. When do you leave for your next shoot?"

As Jake put her down on the opposite bank, her body slid slowly against his. She was having a difficult time thinking. "Next Friday I'm off to photograph the Greek Islands for a couple of weeks. Marta and Nels have agreed to let me live with them when I'm not working."

"You're coming back to Craig?" His emerald eyes revealed a glimmer of light that hadn't been there all day.

"Yes. Does that scare you?"

"No." He paused. "You're really going to live with Marta and Nels?"

"Yes. I was going to rent something in town, but they wouldn't hear of it."

"Why not go back home to California?"

"Because I feel like this is as much my home as California. I have family here and I want to get to know my grandparents better."

"Is that all?" His eyes were probing.

"What do you want me to say?"

A smile broke out as big as the sky. "I'd like you to say you're interested in a guy from Alaska." Then his expression changed. He bent down and kissed her neck. She could feel goose bumps break out on her skin where his lips had touched.

"I'd like you to say you met a ranger who finds you attractive." He cupped her face and softly brushed her lips with his. She felt as if she'd been burned. Her breathing grew shallow from that simple touch.

"I'd like you to say he has a great dog named Beastly."

Sammi's husky laugh died the second their eyes met. Jake's hand reached behind her neck and brought her lips to his in an all-consuming kiss. It felt so natural, so right the way their bodies fit together.

Oh…the way Jake kissed was unlike anything she'd ever experienced. She couldn't get enough. Sammi met him halfway, wrapping her arms around his broad shoulders, holding on to him for support as she gave herself completely to the moment. Unfortunately, it was too short, leaving her breathless and wanting more.

As Jake pulled away, his eyes were glazed with passion and his lips were swollen. It made her feel better to know he was just as affected as she was. She began to trace the rough contour of his jawline, loving how his morning stubble felt.

"Have I said enough, Sam?"

"No. But I like what I've heard so far."

Chapter Six

Sammi marveled how the day had turned out. She sat on one of the wooden chairs on the patio off the Powells' home. The sun shone brightly above the clearing, creating a mirage of glimmering diamonds on the tranquil sea's surface. The brilliant rays brought the various hues of nature to life, with colors she hadn't known existed.

Jake's parents had picked a perfect spot to hold a barbecue. Their home sat on the other side of the cove from her grandparents. The view was glorious. Bald eagles soared above the ring of trees. What amazed her most was the ocean. This evening it was alive with playful porpoises, and sea lions sunning themselves on the small islands.

This was a very different setting than the traditional small-town America celebrating Independence Day. It got Sammi thinking.

What was the ideal American Fourth of July? She thought back to her experience growing up. Wonderful memories of her mother flooded her mind, plus the smell of the vineyard, grapes ripe from the vine, freshly squeezed grape juice, quiche and potato salad.

Sammi could see herself running around the courtyard near the cottage where she and her mother lived. She had a sparkler in her hand, while her mom chased her around with three of them. That was her wonderful, eccentric mother. She'd always been Sammi's friend.

She wondered what her mother was doing on this Fourth with her new husband.

"How was your day of hiking?" Nels asked in his quiet way.

Sammi jumped. "I didn't hear you walk over."

He patted her arm. "You looked lost in thought. The sea has a way of doing that to a person." Her grandpa took a seat next to her and began to eat. He was an amazing man. To think her mom had kept them apart. How was Sammi ever going to put the two halves of her heart back together?

"The hike was beautiful," she said. "There were some bears close by. It scared me a little. Besides that, it was enchanting and pretty much uneventful." The image of Jake kissing her flashed into her mind. She hoped she wasn't blushing. "I'm excited to see the fireworks tonight. What about you, Grandpa? What did you do today?"

"Oh, I went out fishing. For forty years I made my living that way. Had to retire. Arthritis." He tried to make a fist. "But once in a while I find the call of the sea too strong not to go out and do a little bit of it now and again."

She stared at him, thinking he must have been a handsome man when he was young. Now his skin was tough like leather, with wrinkles and sunspots. She could see how that lifestyle had taken its toll. It was written on his face. "I hear fishing is one of the most dangerous jobs in the world."

"Part of a fisherman's pride."

Nels still had spunk. Maybe one day she would do a piece on the fishermen of Craig, Alaska. Spontaneously, she reached over and clasped his shoulder. "I'm so glad I found you." She kissed his cheek, then got up and walked toward the buffet tables before she got too emotional. Tonight was for fun, not tears.

She went over to where the rest of the group was lined up to get their food for the informal party. There were two tables set with red-and-white checkered tablecloths. It was a fish lover's dream, with an assortment of dishes to rival that of the finest restaurants. Sammi loaded her plate with everything. She took a big helping of the potato salad and a large piece of Marta's sour cream apple pie.

"Samantha? How do you stay so thin when you take portions like that?" Doris Powell exclaimed.

"Mom. Be nice." Jake spoke up from behind her. For the last couple of hours Sammi had been waiting to hear his voice. He'd dropped her off at her grandparents so he could do a little work and then clean up.

She turned around to see what a cleaned-up Jake looked like, but Beastly wasn't going to have that. The dog came right up to her, nudging her hand. Sammi always had a soft heart when it came to dogs. She gazed down at the Beast's big brown eyes and gave her a good pat. Then she searched out her owner.

"You look incredible tonight." When Jake bent close and spoke into her hair, Sammi knew she was in trouble. No other guy had the power to make her feel like putty just by the way he talked. She turned around.

Hello! The ranger cleaned up nicely.

He was dressed in jeans and a dark blue polo shirt, filling both out perfectly. The blue of his shirt accentuated his tanned, olive skin. How was she going to handle being close to him? Her friends back at school and at the magazine would die if they saw him. *She* was dying.

"You look pretty good yourself." Heat filled her cheeks.

All of a sudden she wished the Alaskan terrain and climate allowed her something feminine to wear—a pretty summer dress, perhaps. But nope—between the bugs and cool night air, that was never going to happen.

Tonight she was back in staple attire—jeans. She'd done her best to accessorize them with suede boots, a pale blue, long-sleeved shirt and a creamy knit vest lined with faux fur.

"So is this your second or third helping?" Jake teased.

"First." Sammi kept quiet for a moment. "But I have to say I'm looking forward to that pie."

"Sour cream apple. Marta makes the best."

"Don't worry, Jake. I saved you a piece," Marta interjected. "Samantha, dear, you didn't tell me what you two did today."

Sammi glanced over her shoulder at her grandma. Just then Jake decided to rub her back. She was so bemused he answered for her. "We went up to the Harris River." Evidently he knew Sammi wasn't thinking straight. "I'm heading up a research project doing a census on steelhead trout."

The problem was, how could Sammi think when she was around him? This situation was getting complicated. He gave her a wink to let her know he was onto her. He also shot her a look of desire that spoke of what he was really thinking.

She needed some space before she made a complete fool of herself, and headed to the end of the table to grab a drink.

Once everyone was seated, Sammi turned to Doris. "Where's C.J.?"

Everyone stared at her in such a way that she sank back in her chair.

Marta answered for Jake's mother. "Didn't you hear Doug tell us he had to fly back to California early?" Her grandmother couldn't hide the smile on her face.

"I guess I must have missed that." Embarrassed, Sammi stared at her plate and kept eating.

Marta continued to talk. "Well, it *would* make sense. Doug was telling us where he went just as Jake arrived at the barbecue."

Sammi reached for her cup of punch and drank it in big gulps. When she peeked at Jake, he grinned at her while he ate, happy as he could be.

Doris, on the other hand, had started crying. Doug reached over and tried to comfort his wife.

"Mom…" Jake spoke with irritation. "This is something Jeremiah does all the time."

His mother sniffed. "You don't have to look so pleased about it."

"I don't think Jake's glad his brother's in danger," Doug stated.

"Jeremiah lives for this stuff, Mom. His favorite part of the summer is fighting wildfires."

"Son…." his father admonished.

"There's a wildfire in California?" Sammi's heart lurched. Was the vineyard safe? Her mom? "May I ask where?"

"Of course." Doug smiled at her. "No need to worry. It's not where your mother lives. It flared up in the hills near Malibu. Chris just got called in. Fortunately, he was able to catch the last ferry out of here to Ketchikan tonight."

"I'm sorry he had to leave, Doris." Sammi put her half-eaten plate of food on the ground, then straightened. She could hear Beastly licking it up. She didn't really care. She had little appetite tonight, anyway. "I don't blame you for being worried. Last summer I did a piece on wildfires.

"There's one thing I learned when I was out with brave women and men like C.J. They're highly trained and al-

ways put safety first. I've never seen such camaraderie as
on those teams. I'm sure he'll be fine."

For the rest of the meal the Powells asked questions
about her wildfire article. It seemed C.J. had kept them in
the dark, likely to prevent them from worrying too much.
But without him meaning it to, his silence on the subject
had raised their level of anxiety.

As Sammi explained what she'd learned about fire-
fighter teams and how they worked in the field, she hoped
to abate some of Doris's fear. What she hadn't anticipated
was the panic she'd instilled in her grandparents and Jake,
after recounting details of the two-week period she'd spent
getting the spread.

By the time she'd finished talking about it, she found
herself having to calm Jake down. She made him promise
not to call her editor and chew him out for putting her in
danger. "It was *my* idea to take the story," she insisted.

"You sounded like your father just then," Doug com-
mented. Sammi glanced at him, then at her grandparents.
At the moment she couldn't read their faces.

"Are you really that crazy?" Jake snapped. His eyes
held disbelief.

"No, but it was my first chance to get a feature article,
so I took it. My mom already lectured me, for a good three
months at least. Believe me, I've heard about it."

"Sounds like your mama has some sense. Maybe you
should listen to her," Marta interjected.

Sammi was done with all this talk. She decided it was
time to go to the kitchen and help clean up. Jake followed
her, as did everyone else. Half an hour later they had the
Powells' yard and house back in perfect condition. Jake and
his dad headed outside, while the rest of the party went into
the living room to chat.

Jake's mother walked over to Sammi. "Would you like a tour of the house while Jake finishes helping Doug with the boat for a moment?"

"Sure."

Doris headed down the hall, motioning for her to come so she could show her their spacious home. Everywhere Sammi looked there were lighthouses! Jake's mom was truly obsessed. Her home could be a lighthouse museum, with her collection including everything from soap dispensers to light fixtures. Sammi marveled at how many ways one could decorate with that motif.

The room that surprised her most was Doug's den. The walls were covered with photos of the twins and all their accomplishments. Sammi's mom had done that back at the cottage, except that in her mother's case it wasn't just one room—the whole house was filled with pictures of Sammi. It made her wonder if things were kept the same now that Andrea was married to Max.

After one look around the den, Sammi was drawn to the wall dedicated to Jake. While she avidly gazed at the pictures of him, his mother asked, "How did you know this was my Jakey?"

"These photos look like him."

Doris studied her for a moment. "Very few people can tell the twins apart."

"Yes, but here he's playing in the dirt and fishing, and his eyes are a little bigger."

"I'm impressed," the older woman murmured.

Sammi's gaze traveled beyond the pictures. "Look at all these science awards! Is that a Ph.D. in ecology?"

She nodded. "The boys are the first in both Doug's and my line to graduate from college. My Jacob is the brain in the family. We were so proud when he got his doctorate.

C.J. didn't go on past his master's. He could never quite keep up with Jake in that department. The twins are very competitive."

Sammi felt like an idiot. Here she thought she was hot stuff, with a bachelor's from Brooks. Little did she know Jake had three degrees.

"Here's his crowning achievement."

"There's more?"

"I know. He's special." There were a lot of implications in that one word. Sammi picked up on his mom's undertones.

Above Doug's desk hung a plaque that gave all rights of a patent to Jacob Douglas Powell. "What kind of a patent?"

"Mom?" Jake's voice came from the hallway. "You're showing her the wall of shame." He sounded like an embarrassed teen.

Sammi turned around in surprise. "Tell me about your patent."

"Did you have to do this, Mom?" He leaned against the door frame, looking annoyed at his mother. The man was so handsome he almost stole Sammi's breath away.

"I show everyone this room," Doris said defensively. "You know that."

This ranger was more than Sammi had ever bargained for. He was gorgeous, he loved his parents and his job, and he was highly educated. Except she could tell from their conversation earlier today that he had a hard time trusting. What had happened to make him so wary?

He had another imperfection, too. He didn't like to travel. *Just hold on to that thought before he steals your heart, Sammi.*

JAKE TURNED OFF THE MOTOR on the boat. "Do you like it out here, Sam?"

What wasn't there to like?

He'd brought her to a spot in the harbor in his speedboat where they could look at the town of Craig to watch the fireworks. Causeways connected this unique community set on small islands—a fishing village that brought fisherman as well as all types of tourists to its charming shores.

"It's beautiful the way the water is lit up by the town lights—very picturesque. I can't recall the last time I saw so many stars. Funny how I was under the impression that Alaska was the land of the midnight sun."

He took her hand and began to caress it. "That's probably one of the most common comments we get, but you have to realize that here in Craig we're only a thousand miles north of Seattle. As you can see from the clock on the boat, it's almost eleven and it's dark. The sun sets around ten-thirty and comes up around four. We aren't Anchorage. It's like comparing Minnesota to Texas."

"That's another note to put in my article. Alaska is huge and spans different longitudes, getting lighter and lighter the farther north you travel."

"Its weather is unpredictable, too," he added. "When we were little my dad used to bring us out here to watch the fireworks *if* the elements cooperated. Most of the time it rained, but the town always sets off fireworks, anyway."

"Then what did you do?"

"We went into town and tried to see the show from the truck window."

"That sounds cozy. So tell me why Craig does its fireworks on the third of July?"

He chuckled at all her questions, but his amusement soon dissipated and the look that entered his eyes made her knees go weak. She was grateful to be sitting down as he began massaging her shoulders. "Want to come back and sit on the benches with me to watch the fireworks? It's a lot more comfortable."

His lazy smile made her nervous in an exciting kind of way. Sammi had kissed guys before, but she'd never been this attracted. He was going to make a move, she just knew it. But did she want to get involved?

In the future she'd be coming back to get to know her grandparents better. What if this didn't work? What if he broke her heart? She was already mixed up emotionally, and this was happening too fast.

But his touch felt so good and relaxing that when he put his face next to hers, she automatically rubbed her cheek alongside his. "To answer your question, we have fireworks on the third of July because there used to be only one pyrotechnics display on Prince of Wales Island."

He lowered his head to kiss her neck. The feel of lips on her skin drove her crazy.

"There's a town up the coast called Klawock." With his fingers, he brushed her hair aside. "They have dibs on getting fireworks for the Fourth."

Sammi couldn't have talked about Kalk or whatever the town was called, even if she'd wanted to. He was kissing the other side of her neck now.

In a deft movement, he reached over to the boat's sound system and turned on some music. "Let's dance, shall we?"

She murmured something appropriate.

After helping her remove the blankets she'd bundled up in for the journey, he lifted her off the seat. The tune playing was some type of oldies love song.

"Where did you get this music?"

"It's from a radio station in town." Jake's voice turned husky as he gathered her close.

"I like it," she whispered against his neck. She could

hear his breathing growing faster. While Sammi rested one of her arms on his muscular shoulder, he held her other hand close to his heart. Her head barely came to his chin and she could hear the rhythmic beating of his heart as they swayed to the music. The boat helped in the rocking motion. She lost her footing a few times.

He stared down at her. "It seems you don't have sea legs."

"You're right. I'll have to get some if I were ever to achieve my dream of going on an expedition to Antarctica."

"Are you heading there soon?" His eyes pierced hers.

"Heavens, no. It's just a dream, and I'm rambling."

It appeared there'd been enough of that. His lips came down to silence her. This time there was no lead up interlude. Sammi could feel how much he wanted her and his response brought out feelings she didn't know she had.

The fireworks went off and she could hear the booming as they ignited, but neither of them saw the colorful lights exploding in the night sky.

Chapter Seven

"Beastly? Stop barking! Beastly...!" Jake yelled from his pillow, half-asleep. From the bedroom door the dog's wide face and big brown eyes were looking at him.

Jake sat up in bed, scratching his jaw. He needed a good shave before he saw Sam again. Images of kissing her last night came rushing back to him. He'd made plans to take her canoeing up the coast today. There was an estuary he needed to check on for a census report. It was a private place and he intended to continue what she'd stopped last night.

Beastly's barking started up again. She looked at him, then ran to the front door. That's when he heard the knock. "Who's here, girl?" He looked at his alarm clock. It said 6:13 a.m. Jake hadn't gone to bed until one.

He got up and grabbed jeans and a T-shirt off the floor. Maybe it was one of the recruits from the office who didn't think to call the house first. Rookies always assumed everything was an emergency and had to be dealt with now.

"Jake? I'm sorry to wake you up."

"Sam?" She looked and sounded upset. What was she doing here? Did the woman ever *not* look beautiful? "What's wrong, gorgeous?" The need to hold and comfort her overwhelmed him. "Come in."

He tried to take her hand and lead her inside, but she wouldn't let him. "What's wrong?" Jake could feel some of his previous defenses going up.

Sam bit her lip and began looking all around except at him.

"Talk to me."

"Don't be mad," she begged. Her blue eyes pleaded with him. "While we were out last night, my magazine called me. The head photographer, Sanford James, had a bad rock-climbing accident in Yosemite."

"What does that have to do with you?" Jake knew getting mixed up with a girl like her was trouble, but she was irresistible.

"Sanford was supposed to head to the Serengeti for eight weeks to shoot a wildlife spread. He always takes pictures for the cover articles. Now I've been chosen. This is my chance. It will be my picture on the cover of the December edition of the magazine."

He gritted his teeth. "Is that what's important to you? Fame and notoriety?"

"No. This is my job. I told you I would by flying in and out of Craig in between shoots. Sometimes opportunities come up and if you don't take them, they're gone."

His lungs constricted. "What about us?"

"Us?"

"Yeah, us." How could she ask that?

"I thought we were okay," she said nervously.

Jake lowered his head. "I don't know if I can do this."

"Why?" Sam looked devastated. "You knew exactly what I did for a living when you started seeing me."

"I know, but I thought you weren't leaving for another week."

"I never know when I'm going to leave."

"This is all happening so fast, Sam."

"You think I'm not aware of that?"

He knew his comment had gotten to her, but he was hurting at the thought of her being gone for eight weeks. "Who will be going out with you on safari?"

Her face changed and a cool facade replaced the loving, carefree Sam who had filled his empty life.

"I'll be with Tom Bordner, the magazine's top journalist. He's been following a pride of lions for five years and this is the final article on them. The magazine also hires people to drive, cook and help set up camp."

The thought of her being out alone on safari with another man was hard to handle. "I presume he's the type who picks up on every woman he meets."

"Not to my knowledge."

"That's all you're going to say?"

"I think *you've* said enough, and I have to go."

She started to walk toward a truck parked on the road. He hadn't realized Nels had been waiting in the driver's seat, watching them the whole time.

"How are you leaving the island?" Jake called to her. "I can help fly you off."

She turned around, and her hurt expression made him feel horrible. His mind scrambled to think what he could do to change the situation.

"The magazine has arranged for a charter." With that she climbed in the cab and out his life.

SAMMI LEANED AGAINST the wooden veranda, watching the sun set over the magnificent Serengeti. The animals were loud tonight. In the distance she heard lions roar, while the hippos snorted. Down at the watering hole beneath the deck, crocodiles hissed.

For the first time in her life Sammi was homesick. Her

stomach ached and she had trouble eating. This trip had not turned out as she'd imagined.

Of course, working with Tom was the adventure of a lifetime. To track a pride of lions was an incredible experience, but all she wanted to do was go back to Alaska, back to her grandparents, back to Jake. As the sun slipped beneath the horizon, Sammi walked back to her room to call her mom.

She was so confused about Jake, about her life, that she needed to talk to her best friend. This trip had softened her heart. Sammi didn't know if she could ever understand why her mom had done what she did, but she was still her mother, and Sammi needed her now.

She looked at her watch. It would be early morning at the vineyard. She hoped her mother would still be in the cottage. Now that her mom was married, Sammi didn't know her routine.

"Hello?"

When she heard that sweet voice she'd known all her life, her own throat tightened. "Hi, Mom."

"Sammi! It's so good to hear your voice, honey."

Once her mom started talking to her, Sammi broke into sobs. "It's good to hear you, too."

"Are you still in Africa?"

"I'm flying to Alaska tomorrow."

"You're going back there?" Disappointment filled her voice.

"I know it's not what you want, Mom."

"It isn't important what I prefer. I just want you to be happy."

Sammi couldn't control her sobbing. "I'm so homesick."

"Then why don't you come home?"

"Because Alaska's home to me."

There was a silent pause. "You already love it there that much?"

"I can't describe it. But for the first time I feel like I belong somewhere. These last eight weeks here in Africa have been the worst."

"Your grandparents must be wonderful people."

"Well, yeah—didn't you fall in love with their son?"

She could tell her mom was crying now. "Yes, I did."

"You would love Nels. He's so amazing and kind, and he makes you feel safe and comfortable and loved."

"Oh, Sammi—you've just described your father and how he made me feel."

"And Marta is hilarious, with lots of spunk. Remember how you and I used to laugh about why I was so small and had so much energy?"

"I remember everything."

"Well, Marta and I have the same figure. I always wondered why I didn't get your lovely curves."

"I didn't know that." She sniffed. "You're the greatest daughter a mother could have."

Sammi swallowed hard, trying to deal with her emotions. "Mom—I've talked with my editor and he's going to let me do a trial series called 'Undiscovered Alaska,' which would allow me to stay there four months. I told him I'm still dealing with the aftermath of the tsunami and would like to stay in America for a while. He seemed to be okay with the idea."

"That's marvelous, but does that mean I'm not going to see you at all?" Her mother sounded anxious.

"I don't know." Sammi took a deep breath. "I've met a man."

"I knew there was something going on. Tell me what he's like."

The mere thought of Jake brought a smile to her face. "Well, he's a park ranger. Not like Smokey the Bear, though."

Her mom's laughter sounded through the tears. "Is he tall, dark and handsome?"

"Unfortunately."

"Unfortunately?"

"Yeah. It's a lethal combination."

"I know about lethal. Your father was tall, blond and handsome. Now with Max I know all about the dark part."

"Jake's father is dark, too. He was Dad's best friend...."

She heard her mother's sharp intake of breath. "You don't mean Doug?"

"Yeah. He's Doug's son."

"How incredible!"

"It was a shock to everybody."

"I take it you've met him and his family."

"Yes. I ate dinner with them. His mother is obsessed with lighthouses, paintings and knickknacks all of lighthouses. You would hate it." Her mother giggled. "They live in a cove across from Nels and Marta. There are sea lions and porpoises and whales, and bald eagles flying around. It's so beautiful."

"I've never heard you this happy."

"I'm happy just thinking about Jake. I hope I'm capable of making a relationship work."

"If your love is strong enough, you'll manage."

"How are you doing, Mom?"

"Wonderful, but I've been feeling sick lately."

"How sick? Like dying sick?" Sammi felt her heart drop to her feet.

"No, darling. I—I'm pregnant. I've got morning sickness. Before long you're going to be someone's big sister."

Sammi felt as if her whole world was spinning. Not only had her mom remarried, but now she was going to have an-

other child. As happy as Sammi was for her mother, it hurt
to know all this had happened while she'd been gone. Yet
she knew it had been her decision to stay away.

"I'm very happy for you and Max."

"Thank you, darling."

For Sammi, all the hurt of the past few months was
compounded by this new revelation. "I'll call you when I
get to Alaska. Good night, Mom."

She hung up before she started to cry all over again.

THE SALTY BREEZE FELT wonderful against Sammi's hot
skin while she waited to board her flight. She couldn't
wait to go home to Prince of Wales Island. Her grandparents were there. Equally important, so was Jake.

"Sorry about the luggage mix-up, miss."

"What?" She turned around to face a burly airport
worker. She'd been studying the contrast of the bright
green forest against the gray ocean and hadn't heard him
the first time. She was too happy to be back in Alaska, savoring the atmosphere.

"Somehow your luggage ended up in Dallas, Texas. It
will be here tomorrow. We'll fly it out to Craig."

She exhaled a breath and started to laugh. "That's
sounds about right."

"If you'll fill out this form, we'll deliver it to your house."

Sammi took the clipboard and pen. A gust blew in at just
the right time, whipping the paper in her face. She pushed
it down and began putting information on the tedious form.
While she was doing so, she heard someone calling out,
and looked up.

From behind a small floatplane, a mechanic was yelling to the airport worker who'd been helping her. "Go tell
Chief Powell his plane is ready to take off."

"I'll let him know, Ben." The man took her clipboard and headed back to the terminal.

Chief Powell?

Sammi couldn't stop herself; she hurried over to the mechanic across the way. "Excuse me." She tried to put on her most charming smile. The young man gawked at her. "I heard you say this plane is Chief Powell's. Do you mean Jake Powell, the forest ranger from Craig?"

The skinny man stood up, wiping his dirty hands on his overalls. "Yes, ma'am."

"I'm a friend of his, and I was wondering, do you know where he's going? I've been out of the country for a while."

"He's flying out to the Misty Fjords. That's all I know." He was staring at her as if she was the first woman he'd seen in years.

She concocted a plan on the spot. "Do you think you could take a letter to the pilot who was going to fly me out to Craig? I need him to deliver it to my grandparents. I would pay him." The mechanic didn't move. "I'll pay you, too."

"All right."

"Can you give me a minute?"

He nodded.

Sammi pulled her camera bag off her shoulder and took out some paper and a pen to write.

Dear Grandma and Grandpa,
I've gone with Jake to the Misty Fjords. I saw him when I landed in Ketchikan. My luggage got lost, so it should arrive at the house tomorrow. I love you and can't wait to see you when we get back.
Love,
Your granddaughter,
Samantha.

She put the letter in an envelope with a Serengeti lodge logo on it and wrote down her grandparents' address and phone number in case the pilot was too lazy to drive to their place. Lastly, she pulled some money from her purse, stood up and handed the items to the mechanic.

"Could you take this to my pilot? I'm going to go into Ketchikan and shop for a couple of days. I'll arrange to fly out to Craig later."

Sammi watched the mechanic walk into the hangar. She realized this was her only chance. Praying no one noticed her, she climbed into Jake's floatplane. It was a Cessna 310 that seated only six people. She knew that much from her travels around the world.

How did Jake own a plane? She'd love to hear the answer, but right now it didn't matter, because she needed to hide.

Underneath one of his duffels she spied a wool blanket. She reached for it, settled into the backseat and pulled it over her. For once she was grateful for her small size. If Jake didn't look too closely, he wouldn't know she was there until he got in the plane.

Her whole body was trembling with excitement. Though it was wrong of her to sneak onto his plane, the idea of not seeing Jake for another hour was too much to bear. Please let him understand.

He had to.

She was in love.

Hopefully, he was, too.

Chapter Eight

Sammi woke up sick. Before she could say a thing, the aircraft dropped, so fast it took her breath away, and she found herself hitting the ceiling of the plane. "Ouch!"

"What the— Sam?" Jake's voice cried out in a combination of disbelief and anger.

"Jake. My head really hurts."

Sammi lay partly on top of Jake's luggage and partly over the rear seat of the plane. She saw everything double and wasn't sure she could move. Her leg seemed to be stuck.

She heard the sound of Jake unbuckling his seat belt. "Don't do that!" she screamed.

"Don't do what?"

"Leave the cockpit. What if we go through another shear and lose control again?" Sammi fought hard not to break down.

"Listen, Sam," he said in a soothing voice. "I went through the edge of a huge storm that's moving into the area. I never lost control, sweetheart. If I'd known you were in the plane, I would have explained that to you." She could hear him coming closer to her.

"I've traveled in small planes. They don't have autopilots."

"Well, this one does. I put it in a couple of years ago."

She felt a weight being lifted off her leg. The pain subsided, thank heaven. "What was that thing pinning me down?"

"My luggage," he replied brusquely. She felt his hand touch her leg through her jeans. It had a calming effect.

"Mmm. That feels nice. I've missed you, Jake."

"Sam? I need you to move your leg. Can you do that?"

"I think so." She lifted it and bent it in all the directions he asked her to.

"I imagine you'll have a nasty bruise, but it appears to be okay." He was throwing things on the floor, clearing a space. Once he'd made room, he proceeded to check the rest of her body.

He asked her to move her fingers, making her feel like a guinea pig. Then his hands encircled her neck and he lifted her head to look at her. There was no way to describe the intensity of those eyes as he checked to make sure it was safe to move her.

While she lay there in a daze, he sat in the space he'd cleared. Next he gently slid his arms beneath her neck and legs, and in one quick motion cradled her against his body.

Being so close to Jake again, Sammi thought she'd gone to heaven. Nothing compared to the feeling of being in his arms. He pressed her face into his neck, and she felt his breath on her hair. This was what it was like to feel safe. It had been so long since she'd seen him.

"Sam? I need you to look at me."

She didn't want to leave the cocoon of his embrace. All she wanted to do was go to sleep. "I'd rather rest."

Jake wouldn't let her do any of those things. He pulled away, cupping her face in his hands. He was so handsome. She loved him in his uniform. "You're one sexy ranger. I'm going to call you Smokey because you're so hot." She leaned in and kissed him. Jake didn't turn away, but he wasn't as responsive as usual.

"What's wrong? Don't you like me anymore?" Sammi could feel herself getting emotional.

His expression was full of worry. "Oh, I like you all right, but I don't take advantage of women who are hurt. You have a concussion."

"Really?"

"Your pupils are dilated and your head is bleeding."

Sammi felt with her hand, and cringed when she saw the bloody mess on her fingers. She quickly wiped them on her jeans. "I think I hit my head."

"Yes, you did." His expression remained impassive. He reached over and opened the first-aid kit hanging on the side of the plane. With some gauze and bandages, he stopped the bleeding. By the time he'd finished, she was sure she resembled a war patient. "I must look hideous. Like when Van Gogh cut off his ear."

He suppressed a laugh. "Van Gogh, huh?"

"My mom really liked his work. We had lots of sunflowers at the vineyard. I always remembered the story of him cutting off his ear. *Now* look at me. I'm Van Gogh." She was pathetic. "I'm not pretty."

"You could never be anything but beautiful. You're hurt, but it doesn't mean you're not attractive." His green eyes bored into hers and she leaned in and kissed him again.

"Is it hot in here? Maybe it's being next to you, Smokey. It's making me hot." She clumsily removed her jacket. Jake ended up helping her. She kept trying to kiss him, which made things more difficult.

Her short-sleeved T-shirt had a big, smiling hippo and the message Kiss Me. "Do you like my shirt?" She smiled, trying for another kiss.

"Why didn't you come in the hangar and ask me to take you along?"

Sammi snuggled against him, rubbing her face against his, bandages and all. "After I left for Africa, I didn't think you wanted to see me again." She loved the feel of his freshly shaved face, the smell of his aftershave, but she still wasn't close enough. "I had a lot of stuff to tell you, so I sneaked aboard so you couldn't get rid of me." She started kissing his neck. Then she tried to kiss his lips.

"Samantha!" He pulled away from her abruptly and put his hand on her forehead. His cool touch felt delicious. "You're burning up with fever."

"I'm burning for you, Smokey."

"You have no idea what you're even saying."

Jake sounded gruff. He carried her to the front passenger seat and strapped her in. It was a pain because he wouldn't let her go to sleep. He kept nudging her awake. She could hear him talking to her and then to somebody else, but it was very confusing to know when to answer. His conversation came in bits and pieces.

"I'm going to set down at Winstanley Island and seek refuge at the cabin there. I have some medical supplies on board, but she'll need antibiotics and medical help as soon as possible.

"Contact Doc Stevens and get him ready to fly out once the storm clears. Forward a message to the Engstroms. Tell them I have Samantha with me in the Fjords…. How long do you think the storm will last? Over and out."

JAKE HEARD THE DOCTOR'S floatplane before it landed on the picturesque waters near the shore of Winstanley Island. He was still shaking when he thought of Sam hitting the ceiling of the plane. What he couldn't comprehend was her stealing on board like that, but it didn't matter now.

He ran a hand along his jaw, trying to calm down. The most important thing was that he and Sam had made it safely to the forest service cabin before the snow hit. Luckily, the forecasters had been wrong and the storm was headed north.

Though he'd given her ibuprofen, she was still burning up with fever. He didn't know what more he could do, and was grateful Doc Stevens had come to check on her. They'd been friends since their undergrad studies in Anchorage. Cole owed him big time with all the sticky situations the doctor seemed to get himself into. He was always radioing Jake to help him get people out of the worst of circumstances.

One thing about Cole, he'd do anything to help a patient. Some rescuers wouldn't touch the remote areas Jake ventured into. But Doc Stevens took the Hippocratic oath to an extreme.

Jake knew the reason for it. Cole and his brother had gone on a backcountry ski trip and had been caught in an avalanche. His brother was killed instantly, and Cole was forced to wait forty-eight hours alone in the Alaskan wilderness with a broken leg before he was rescued. After that experience he vowed he'd never let someone be alone and in pain if he could help it.

He was now known as Doc Stevens, the Alaskan Bush Doctor. He loved all the women he could woo with his exciting lifestyle, *when* he could find them. But he wasn't getting Sam!

Cole stepped out of the plane onto the cabin dock. "Powell—did you have to give a girl a concussion to get her alone in the wilderness?"

For perhaps the first time Jake realized that his friend

was a good-looking guy. Tall with blond hair and a large frame, he looked suave in his preppy mountain wear. Would Sam think the same thing?

"Better than your brash 'doctor hero' approach."

"So what happened?"

Jake explained as they walked up to the cabin.

"Stop," he said as Cole reached for the door. "There's one more thing."

His friend chuckled. "I've never seen you so tied up in knots before."

"She's not acting like herself."

"Right, a concussion and high fever. You and I went to paramedic school together. You already know all this stuff. This girl has you so wound up I think *you* need a doctor."

"She's been calling me Smokey."

His pal broke into laughter and slapped him on the back, but Jake wasn't in the mood for joking. "Right now she's extremely affectionate and I don't want you to think she's that type of girl. She's not!"

Their eyes met. In a more serious tone Cole said, "You've fallen for her."

"Maybe."

"I never thought I'd see the day Jake Powell would switch feelings from Beastly to a woman. Now I've got to meet the female who calls you Smokey. Like the bear?"

"She claims it's because I'm so hot."

More laughter rolled out of Cole as he followed him inside the cabin, then he let out a low whistle. "She's pretty hot herself."

"I'm watching you, Stevens." Jake knew he sounded uptight, but he didn't care. She always made his heart race.

Sam was lying on the cot with her hair splayed over the pillow. She'd pulled the compress off her head, revealing a glimpse of her perfect profile. She still wore her hippo T-shirt. He'd put her into a pair of his pajama bottoms and had covered her with a sheet.

"I like the shirt," Cole teased.

"So does she."

He went about checking her vitals and temperature. "She might have malaria. Let's get on the phone to her magazine, her doctor and the team she worked with in Kenya."

Two hours later the malaria was ruled out. She'd been careful to take her medication.

"Jake? Turns out she has a bad bug and a minor concussion. She's going to be fine. If you weren't so involved, you'd be able to see that."

"She hit her head on the ceiling of my Cessna, Cole. It scared the daylights out of me. Thought I might lose her."

At that revelation Cole went out to his plane and brought back a couple of bags of IV antibiotics. "Since you're trained, I'm going to have you give her this medicine. I'd rather not move her if we don't have to."

Cole drew some blood to take back with him in case there was something he'd missed. Then he inserted the IV in her hand. "She should be fine in a day or so. While I pack up, will you run out to the plane and get some extra tubing?"

"Anything else?" Jake barked. "Laundry? Coffee? A beer?" He stomped out of the cabin, hating being ordered around.

"JAKE, I'M THIRSTY AND HOT." Sammi slowly sat up and glanced around. She took one look at the stranger and frowned. "You're not Jake. Where is he?"

"I'm Dr. Stevens, a friend of Jake's. Can I examine you now that you're up?"

Tears welled in her eyes. "Where's Jake? Where am I?"

"You're in Alaska, in the Misty Fjords. You have a fever from a bug you caught in Africa. Can I look in your eyes, Samantha?"

"No. I want Jake. I want my Smokey."

Jake came through the door. "Why is she crying, Stevens?" he demanded.

"Jake—"

He came and sat down next to her. "I'm here."

Sammi was so happy he was back, she climbed right onto his lap. "Why do I have an IV?" She fell against his chest, wanting to go to sleep again. He began to massage her back and play with her hair.

Cole cleared his throat. "I'd like to check her now that she's awake, and see what kind of concussion she's sustained."

After ten minutes of prodding, they got Sammi to cooperate enough to rule out anything major. By the time they were done, she'd fallen asleep in Jake's arms. He laid her on the cot, careful not to jar the IV.

"Walk me out to the plane, Jake. I don't think she'll wake up for a while."

The two men headed out of the cabin into the rugged paradise surrounding them.

"I've never had a woman take such a dislike to me before." Cole rolled his eyes. "That girl is crazy about you. How did you manage that, Powell?"

"My concern now is to figure out how to keep her."

"Oh, I think you'll find a way, Smokey," he teased before he climbed into his plane.

"One day it's going to happen to you, Stevens."

"Oh, no. I like my freedom."

"That's what we all say until we meet the right one."

Cole ignored his comment. "Radio me if you need anything, lover boy."

Jake shut the door to the plane and jumped back on the town dock.

SAMMI WOKE UP with a dull headache and a throat so dry it felt like a desert. She couldn't open her eyes. It took her a moment to realize she had a compress on her head. With a weak hand, she reached up to remove the cool washcloth. Then she sat up in her cot. Where was she?

The tiny cabin was cozy, with a fire blazing in the woodburning stove. There was another cot right next to hers. Jake!

It all came flooding back to her—the plane, the wind shear and the accident. What a fool she'd made of herself. Sammi reached up and felt a bandage on her scalp. "Did I really call him Smokey?" she muttered to herself.

"I believe it's because I'm so hot."

She turned to see her rescuer standing larger than life in the doorway. In a flannel shirt and jeans, he looked as if he belonged here in this rustic cabin. Humiliated, she groaned, "Did I really say that?"

"I can elaborate if you'd like."

Sammi studied his inscrutable expression to see what he thought of her actions. Had she ruined everything? She bit her lip, terrified of the consequences. No matter what, she had to face them.

Jake walked into the cabin, letting the door slam. The noise made her jump. She saw a hint of mirth in his eyes. Hopefully, he wasn't too mad.

"How are you feeling?" he asked.

"Do you want the lie or the truth?" Sammi propped her hands on either side of her.

"The truth." He moved closer, making her stomach flutter.

"Horrible."

"Considering what you've been through, I'm not sur-prised." He sat down on her cot and lifted her chin. His touch made her breathing shallow.

Their eyes met and she knew why the eight weeks away had been torture for her. More importantly, she knew why she wasn't going to leave anymore. Sammi hoped she could make her four-month trial for the magazine work so she could stay here in Alaska.

In Africa she'd carried a photo of Jake on her at all times, like a moonstruck teenage girl. Now she realized no photo could replace him in the flesh. He needed a shave and his hair was unruly, but that's what she loved about him. He didn't have to primp. Jake was all male.

Sammi raised her hand to his cheek, letting her fingers explore his arresting features. "Thanks for taking such good care of me." At her touch he closed his eyes, not pull-ing away. It made her more daring. She brought her other hand up to trace his full lips with her fingertips. Then his eyes opened, and the look he shot her sent electricity through her whole being.

He pulled her into his arms, crushing her against him. With just a kiss he took possession of her body and soul. Sammi couldn't get enough. Jake had never been this bold, running his hands up into her hair and down her back. Somehow the kiss seemed to melt away the eight weeks of separation. As their bodies clung, their kiss grew deeper.

Jake laid her back on the cot and followed her down. His lips never left hers. Sammi struggled to stay awake. The world started to spin and she grew light-headed. As he kissed her neck, she turned her face away. "Jake? I think I'm going to pass out."

Chapter Nine

Jake realized he had to get control of himself. *Don't attack the poor girl the second she comes out of her fever.*

Now that he knew Sammi had awakened, he couldn't bear to leave her side. Hell, since Cole's visit three days ago, Jake had left the cabin only long enough to get the bare necessities, retrieve water, do some fishing and chop wood.

He sat in his old camping chair, resting his face in his hands. When he left this cabin, he planned on burning the chair, since he never wanted to sit this much again.

A sudden movement caused him to look up. Sammi had opened her eyes, pulling him from his thoughts.

Weighted with guilt, he said, "I'm sorry, Sam."

She sat up, quirking her brows. "For what?"

He rubbed his eyes. "You've been sick and I took advantage of you."

Sammi gave him a teasing look. "Oh, I think it was pretty mutual." She swung her legs over the side of the cot and began to stretch. "Is there anything to drink?"

Her voice sounded so weak. Then she had to start biting her lip in that adorable way…. Thinking of her mouth, Jake leaped out of the chair.

"There's coffee or water. If you're hungry we have some

freeze-dried food to eat." He pointed to some boxes in the corner. "I can fix you something right now or you can wait until I catch dinner."

"Just water, thanks."

He handed her a bottle before walking to the other side of the room to get his fishing tackle. Jake needed to put some distance between them. His mind was filled with so many thoughts and questions to ask her, but she'd just gotten up. He couldn't do that to her yet.

Her soft tread reached his ears. Her presence in the cabin was driving him wild. Her smell, the sound of her voice— and now she was awake. Against his better judgment he followed her progress across the room. How could a woman look so incredible in a huge T-shirt and oversize pajama bottoms? His body trembled at her approach.

"I've got to go catch some dinner. I'll be outside on the shore. If you need me, holler." He grabbed his tackle and pole and was out the door before he did anything stupid, like take her back to the cot and kiss the daylights of out her.

THE SECOND THE DOOR SHUT, all the emotion Sammi had kept bottled up for weeks exploded in a gush of tears. She'd made such a mistake.

All she'd done was make his life miserable. He probably had work to do and now he'd been forced to take care of her for who knew how long?

Sammi walked over to her camera bag, the one thing in the room she owned. Bending down, she pulled the camera out to see the date.

"It can't be!" She shot up and looked through the lens again. She'd been out of it for *four days!* After putting the camera back in the case, she sank down on the cot. How could that be?

No wonder Jake was so tense. Here he'd been a gentleman, taking care of her, and what did she do? Wake up and throw herself at him, then pass out when he kissed her. How humiliating!

Sammi scrambled to find her one outfit, folded tidily in a corner. She changed into her jeans and T-shirt. An hour later, after she'd managed to eat some soup and clean herself up, she threw on her jacket and went outside to talk to Jake like a normal person. She hoped she could face him without feeling too weak.

Once out the door, she found the magic of the Misty Fjords stopping her in her tracks. She'd already been entranced by Alaska, but this natural wonderland was beyond description. It was automatic for her to run back to the cabin and get her camera.

The sun was starting to set in a semicloudy sky. Like sentinels, the forested mountain peaks jutting out of the sea were haloed in clouds. The sun's last rays lit up the mist on the mountains, infusing the vapors with hues of pale yellow and gold. They added an ethereal beauty to this heaven on earth.

Yet to Sammi the most breathtaking view of all was the picture Jake made while he fly-fished. He had a way of melding into the scenery. She stood on the porch, snapping pictures of the man she loved. Whatever type of fish he caught, she was sure he could tell her its name, habitat, what it ate, and how to filet and cook it.

Just then a bald eagle flew overhead, back to its nest. Sammi followed its progress, noticing that it landed close to the cabin. She had heard their nests were the largest in the world. Wanting a peek at this natural marvel, she ventured into the woods.

"Where are you going, Sam?" Jake's surly tone brought her back to reality, making her flinch.

Rats! The last thing she'd wanted to do was make him mad. She whirled around and saw him standing just a few feet from her in his waders. How he moved so quickly in those things was a mystery. "You got here fast."

In the minute it took him to find his voice, his face took on a myriad of expressions. The longer he didn't say anything, the worse Sammi felt. She hated silence, but for some reason, she knew she shouldn't say a word.

He was upset, and after everything she'd put him through, she thought it better not to open her mouth.

"We need to set up a few rules for safety." His jaw was so taut she thought it might crack.

"Okay."

"Come down to the shore with me while I finish up."

"But there's this amazing bald eagle with a nest just a little way behind the cabin. How about I go take the picture and we'll talk after you do your fishing?"

"No!"

"No? You're not my boss, Jake. I've always wanted to see a bald eagle's nest. They're supposed to be huge."

His face was implacable. "Tell me something I don't know."

Ouch. She just kept ruining everything. Better to humor him until she flew out of here. Then she could leave him alone and somehow put her life back together. Not tempting fate again, she walked toward the calm waters.

"I tend to get carried away, taking pictures," she explained. "What did you want to talk to me about?"

Jake didn't say a word. He just moved ahead of her at a clipped pace.

Stupid, hot ranger.

Why did she have to fall for a guy like him? She stopped halfway down to the shore, pretending to take a picture of the scenery while she struggled to get her feelings in check.

Could Jake have kissed her like that in the cabin and not care for her? Last July he'd told her he did. Maybe he'd met someone else since then. Her heart lurched at the thought of him being with another woman.

Sammi sat down on the rocky ground, not able to breathe. Pain constricted her chest. What if he didn't love her? She'd always heard of unrequited love. How did you get over someone like Jake Powell?

Her body was still weak. She knew she was pathetic, but she was so in love, she had to find out how he felt.

Jake was packing up, putting most of his fishing gear in the plane. As she questioned his actions, it dawned on her. Bears. He had a pot in his hand probably full of fish he'd prepped out here, away from the cabin.

"Sam? Are you okay?" His voice sounded worried. *Good.* It should sound worried. He couldn't kiss her, be mean to her, then walk outside and do what he wanted without some explanation.

His hard expression had softened. "What happened? Did you hurt yourself, or are you feeling sick again? I can get us loaded up and fly you to a hospital within the hour, now that you're walking."

It wasn't fair that a man could look so incredible; he matched the perfection of nature. Pain made her cry out, "Is that what you want, to get rid of me? I'm sorry I sneaked onto your plane and ruined your trip. Chalk it up to a girl who fell in love with a dream. Please take me back to Craig."

Sammi stood up and turned back to the cabin.

"Oh, no, you don't—" Jake put the pot down and grasped her hand, drawing her toward him. "Don't I get to say anything?" When he gazed down at her, his expression had changed again. There was a new light in his eyes.

"What is it?" She'd lost hope for salvaging anything between them.

"You don't say something like that and walk away, Samantha Danbury. At least not to me."

He pulled her close, resting his chin on the top of her head. His hold on her was so tender, it gave her an inkling of hope. Those hands slowly began to massage her back, and she couldn't resist wrapping her arms around him.

There'd been a magnetic pull between them since she'd first laid eyes on the man. When their bodies were this close, the sensation had a way of washing away reason. All she could do was react, savoring the power of his touch.

Jake's fingers caressed her neck and played with her hair. She could feel his heart race as he placed kisses in the hollow of her throat. His lips brushed her ear, and Sammi felt her knees go weak. "I'm in love with you, Sam."

She lifted her head so she could look him in the eye. As their gazes met, she could see he wasn't lying. In his was desire, but also affection. She'd seen it before, when she'd awakened from her fever this afternoon.

"You haven't answered me," he muttered. "How do *you* feel?" Jake was getting ready to pull away from her. Sammi wasn't going to have that.

She found her first real smile since leaving for Africa. "I'm in love with you, too."

Jake didn't need to hear anything else. He supported the back of her head and kissed her so intimately, all she could do was respond. It was all she wanted to do.

She had no idea long they stood out there, but when he lowered her feet to the ground, she didn't think she could walk back to the cabin. Her lips were swollen and she was a little dizzy from his kisses. "How come you never kissed me like that before?"

"Are you asking for more?" He winked, then picked up the pot of fish.

"Absolutely."

"Later. Right now you're still recovering from being sick, and I've got to get this fish cooking before I draw every bear in the area to our cabin."

She started back, but wobbled and tripped, finding she had little strength left. Jake came up from behind and picked her up as if she weighed nothing. Normally she would hate being carried around, but today she was exhausted, and if she was honest, she loved being close to him for any reason. "I love you, Jake."

"I love you, too."

Sammi rested her head against his shoulder, feeling utterly whole, peaceful, happy and loved.

Chapter Ten

"Wake up, sleepyhead."

Sammi sat up in her cot and rubbed her eyes. "What happened?"

"You fell asleep."

"How long this time?"

"Just an hour."

"Oh." She looked around the room. "What are you cooking? It smells delicious."

"We're having sockeye salmon steaks. They come from a big boy I tagged two years ago. He's grown even bigger since the last time I saw him."

"Did you name him, too?"

That's when Sammi noticed the makeshift table he'd prepared. Touched by his thoughtfulness, she felt bad for teasing him.

"It looks fabulous," she added. He gave her an infectious smile before gathering her in his arms to claim another kiss. "What I meant to say was, how did you know you tagged him?"

"Sit down and I'll tell you." He pulled out one of the camping chairs for her and put her metal plate on the box he'd used for their table. Water bottles were the drink of choice, placed to the right, with plastic utensils adding the finishing touch.

He took a seat across from her. It was the most perfect dinner she could ever have imagined. A romantic glow filled the room from the front of the wood-burning stove. Sammi was starving and the meal looked divine. He'd made rice to go with the salmon. *Delicious.* She took a couple of bites before she realized she was being rude.

"This meal is incredible. Thank you."

"Glad you like it."

They ate in a comfortable silence. That was something Sammi was getting used to with Jake. She didn't always have to fill in gaps or make small talk. Sometimes silence said more than words. Every time Jake looked at her, she felt her heart leap a little. She was positive the air was alive with the electricity between them.

Once finished with her food, she said, "You never told me how you knew about this salmon. What did you call him? Oh, yeah—big boy."

Jake grabbed his water bottle and sat back in his chair. "Sam, what I'm going to tell you is off the record."

She didn't understand. "In what way?"

"I didn't mean to sound cryptic. Come over here." He crooked his finger at her.

Sammi shook her head.

"I'll come and get you."

"I'd like to see that."

"Sam…"

She got up and stood in front of him. "What do you want me to do?"

He toppled her into his arms. "I can't seem to get enough of you tonight."

"Just tonight?" she teased.

"No." A sound of exasperation escaped his chest. "Will you stop dissecting all my words and just let me talk?" He gave her a kiss that made them both forget what they were discussing.

She snuggled against his chest. "I love how fast your heart beats when we kiss."

"Why?"

"Because you're so much bigger than I am. It's fun to know I have some kind of power over you."

Jake cupped her face. "You have more than that—you have my heart."

"And you have mine."

He held her so tight she thought she wasn't going to be able to breathe.

"When I was working on my doctorate, I figured out a way to tag fish in a safe and cost-effective way, and have been doing it ever since. When I caught this fish this evening, I ran a scanner over it, and sure enough, it had the Powell tag."

She sat up. "It's something special, right?"

Jake lips twitched. "Yeah."

"Do a lot of reserves and scientists use it?"

"Yes."

Sammi cocked her head. "I remember the plaque for your patent hanging in your dad's den. Is that why you have such a nice house on the mountain for a ranger?"

"You noticed?"

"I didn't mean to. I wasn't there that long, and then you hurt my feelings and I tried not to like you."

"Tried not to like me?" He smiled and started kissing her jawline. "What about loving me?" His hands moved over her back again, driving her to distraction.

"I couldn't help that," she confessed.

"Me, either."

Sammi slid her arms around his neck. "So out of curiosity, why are you a ranger? If you have money and are brilliant, you could obviously do a lot more academically."

"I have all a man could ever want right here. I get to use my invention and live in nature doing what I love, with the added benefit of not having to worry about money."

"You're a fortunate man."

He stared at her. "I am now. When I get you back home, there's something we have to do together. Consider it a special gift from me."

"I can't wait! How soon are we leaving?"

"Tomorrow."

SAMMI CLUNG TO JAKE. "How did you know we would fit in a one-man kayak?"

"It's *my* kayak. It's not like we're going paddling for miles and miles."

In reality she barely fit in front of him, but Jake didn't mind. He loved having an excuse to hold her close.

"Can I take my blindfold off yet?"

"In a minute."

Jake couldn't believe their luck. It was rare to have a clear sky in the fjords. The aurora borealis was in full swing tonight, lighting up the sky in all its brilliance. One of the magical elements of living in Alaska—the sky was always alive. Now that it was September, the sky would be colorful for months, enchanting visitors and locals at night. He turned the kayak around and set down his paddle. Then he leaned back and nestled Sam closer to him.

"All right. Let's get this thing off."

He couldn't wait to hear her reaction. As a photographer, she would be in awe. The sight inspired him every time he came out here and saw it like this.

"Is that... Oh, my...Jake—" she cried. "I've never seen anything so gorgeous in my life! Thank you so much for this!"

After she'd taken in the wonder for several minutes, he heard her remove the cap from her camera, make a few adjustments and start shooting.

The sky was on fire, with reds, blues and whites all racing along in a miraculous dance. For the next hour or so he answered her questions about the northern lights and the fjords.

"This is the perfect shoot for my launch article."

"What do you mean?"

"It's the reason I came out here. Why I hid on your plane."

His spirits plummeted. "You came out here for an article?" Not for him? All along he'd known he couldn't trust her, yet he'd still fallen for her. Her words crushed him.

"Jake Powell—before you jump to conclusions and get mad again, just listen to me!" She tried to turn around in the kayak, but he was done listening. There was always something with her. He reached for his paddle.

"Jake!" she suddenly cried out again. "What was that? Are there sharks up here?" Her body had started trembling.

He hated it that this woman always tugged at his heart. She was probably trying to distract him, but when he turned his head, he could see they had company swimming next to the kayak.

"It's a pod of whales—orcas. You've probably heard them called killer whales. It's actually a rare sight. The lights must be drawing them up."

"Really?" She looked over the side of the craft cautiously. "Will they tip us over?"

"No."

"Why are you so mad at me?" Her voice sounded tremulous.

"Because everything about you never seems to be what it is."

"Is that what you truly believe? When I told you I loved you, did you think that was a lie?"

He took in a deep breath, not knowing what to say. Hell, he didn't know what to believe. "I think you love me as much as you can. But I don't think you know what you want."

Sam shuddered again.

He felt like a cad, but he was hurting, too. Loving this woman had been a mistake from the beginning. She was a traveling photographer. "You're an adventurer always looking for the next story. I'm a ranger who hopes never to leave America."

"What if I told you I'm not going anywhere? I got permission from my editor to work on a trial piece called 'Undiscovered Alaska' for four months. I hated the idea of being separated from you, so I'm staying in Alaska to see if our relationship can work."

Sam...

Once again he'd jumped the gun, and been cruel to her in the process. But after that explanation, not anymore.

"I have been suffering from the aftermath of the tsunami and the horrors it left behind. I can't ever do that again. Do you have anything to say, Powell?"

There were no words. He reached down and pulled her up onto his lap. She looked so fantastic out here in the Alaskan night, and she was going to be staying. For now all he could do was bend down and kiss her. The brilliance of the heavens couldn't match the joy he felt with her in his arms.

JAKE'S TRUCK WOUND DOWN the country road leading to the Engstrom house. The loud noise reminded Sammi they were back in civilization. Though she was thrilled to see Marta and Nels, she hated to be parted from Jake.

All too soon they pulled up in the drive. "I'll be by around seven to pick you up for dinner," he said.

"Can't wait."

As Jake jumped out of the truck to help her down, Sammi saw her grandparents run out of the house. Until now she hadn't realized how much she'd missed them. Her mom, too… She wished she was bringing Jake home to meet her mother. She would love him.

Sammi's heart continued to be torn in two. Now that her mom was married and pregnant, where would Sammi fit?

When Jake opened the door, he saw her distress and leaned in. "What's wrong?"

"I just miss my mom and I'm happy to see Marta and Nels. I don't know what brought it on."

Jake reached in and gave her a big kiss that took her mind off of everything. By the time he was through, she felt warm all over. "Don't forget, seven." He waved to her grandparents, who stood gaping at them, and then drove off.

"EVENING, NELS. Is Sam ready?" Jake couldn't wait to see her. The past five hours away from her had felt like an eternity.

The older man's face looked strained. "Give her another five minutes and she will be. Why don't you come in, son? Sam is talking to someone who came up here to see her."

Jake followed him into the house, sensing something was wrong.

"Nels?" Marta called from the kitchen.

"Yes?"

"When Sam comes in, will you tell her that her boss needs her to call him back? They've been trying to reach her. The two main sponsors at the magazine are considering pulling out if she isn't the photographer on the Antarctica expedition."

What?

Suddenly Jake could feel his whole world crashing down around him. Sam was going to Antarctica? And who in the hell was she talking to? He turned to Nels. "Where are they?"

"Out in back, but take it easy, son. It's not what you think. Jake—" He followed him. "Before you go out there, you need to listen to me."

Jake could hear him, but couldn't stop. Deep down, he'd always known Sam was too good to be true. He headed around to the back of the house, where he spied an unfamiliar car. When he saw a tall, good-looking man dressed in an expensive suit speaking heatedly with the woman he loved, jealousy such as he'd never known raged through him.

He could tell by their body language they weren't getting along. A few steps closer and he heard Sam say, "It's time for you to leave. Jake will be here soon and I don't want him to meet you."

Well, that said it all! Jake had seen and heard enough. He stormed back to his Jeep and drove off.

As SAMMI KNOCKED on Jake's door, she felt a strong sense of déjà vu. His home was much larger than she remembered from that morning two months ago. It was a big cabin-style house, built into the rugged hillside and offering breathtaking views of the cove.

Her heart was pounding so hard she thought it might burst. Why hadn't her mother just come out and said how much she wanted to see Sammi? How much she was missed by everyone at the vineyard? She couldn't help it if she'd been in Africa and then sick out in the fjords. And she'd never received the invitation about Steve and his ex-wife getting remarried.

Max didn't have to come up here and chew her out. He wasn't her father and he needed to stop acting like one. She and her mom could have discussed this on the phone. They could have cleared it up so easily. Now it had turned into a disaster.

What hurt most was that Jake had so little trust in her. He'd taken off at the first sight of her with another man. Little did he know Max was her mother's husband. He'd flown up to Craig on a private charter. Only *he* could afford to come all the way here to chew her out.

Sammi rapped on the door again. She could hear Beastly barking, and then the door opened. She wasn't prepared for the sight that met her. Jake was in his ranger outfit, a duffel bag on the floor next to him. In his hand was a gun. He looked absolutely forbidding. The Jake she'd come to know and love was gone, replaced by somebody else.

She barely had the courage to speak. "Why did you leave my grandparents' house?"

He shot her a look that made her feel so insignificant, she had to back away. "I didn't want to intrude on you and your boyfriend."

How could he think that of her?

"It's time for you to leave, Sam."

Sammi thought the day she'd found the journal had been the worst day of her life. She was wrong. Today her entire world was disintegrating. Everyone she loved besides her grandparents had betrayed her.

"You won't even let me explain?"

Jake picked up his duffel. "I always knew you were trouble. Tonight just proved me right. Have fun in Antarctica. Goodbye." With those words, he shut the door.

THE RAIN CAME DOWN in a drizzle and the fish weren't biting. Jake threw another empty beer can on the deck of his boat, adding to the growing pile. It had been two months since he'd closed the door on Samantha and he still couldn't get her out of his mind.

He was haunted by the smell of her skin, the coy look in her blue eyes and the way her hair would blow in the wind. By now she was on the other side of the world, with someone else. The thought of another man holding her, kissing her perfect lips…

"Dammit."

He threw down his fishing pole to go get another beer. That's when he spotted Beastly skulking on the stairs. She poked her head out of the galley. "Come here, girl." She came on command, letting him pet her.

Just as Jake started opening a can of food for her, the dog began to bark. She ran to the far side of the boat, which was pointing in a southerly direction. He walked over to see what Beastly was barking about. This late in the season there were few tourists in the area. This spot was a secret only a few Alaskans knew about. Either someone was lost or Jake was needed. He shouldn't have turned off his radio.

Soon he could see it was Nels's boat approaching. He hoped nothing was wrong with his family or the Engstroms. *Or Sammi.* A shiver of fear coursed through him. Nels didn't often venture out to find people.

The older man put his boat into idle and threw buoys over the side so he could moor it next to Jake's. "I was going to ask permission to come aboard, but your ship is filthy. So are you. When was the last time you shaved, son?"

Jake pulled the hood of his jacket down and ran a hand through his hair. Maybe the cool rain falling on his face would help him get control of his temper. He didn't need anyone else getting after him. His parents had done enough of that. "Do you mind telling me what brings you up to Bucareli Bay?"

Nels turned off his engine, then looked at Jake with such disdain it made him take a step backward. Some of the cans lying on the deck crunched underfoot.

"Why don't you come down and have some of Marta's homemade chili with me? It's not a request." He headed to his galley, making Jake feel he had no choice but to follow. Jake told Beastly to stay, and she happily trotted back to her bed below deck.

By the time he made it down the stairs Nels was dishing up the food. Jake took off his jacket and hung it on a hook, then took a seat at the tiny table, squishing his legs into the tight space.

Nels placed their lunch in front of them and ate with him in silence. Jake didn't feel hungry, but he respected Nels, so he ate. Before long he was on his third helping.

"You've lost a lot of weight."

"I've been busy."

Nels nodded. "You're acting like a jealous teenager who knows nothing and is taking his anger out on everyone else. I don't care what you do to yourself, son, but I do care how you treat my Sammi."

"I don't recall asking for your opinion." Jake had taken enough of this and started to get up.

"Sit down. I'm not done. I didn't travel all the way up here for nothing."

This was a side of Nels he'd never seen before. He decided to let the old man finish what he'd come here to say.

"The day Sammi was flying home from Africa, she was asked to fly down to California to attend the wedding of

Steve de Roussillac and his ex-wife. They were the people that let Sammi and her mother live at the vineyard and have a decent life. Steve has been like a father figure to her. We tried to get the news to you, but then Cole radioed us per your request, letting us know how sick she was.

"Marta and I decided to tell her when she got home. The man you saw Sammi talking to is Max de Roussillac, her mother's husband. He came up on his own accord to find out why Sammi didn't fly down for the wedding. They haven't exactly been friends in the past, but that's another story."

Her mother's husband? Jake reeled from the news. He'd never let Sammi explain. When he thought of how he'd treated her, what he'd done, he felt ill.

"Explain to me why they don't get along?"

"Max is the son of Steve de Roussillac, the owner of the vineyard where Sammi grew up. As she put it, 'He's a jerk and not worthy of her mother.'"

Jake dropped his head in his hands. "I remember her talking about him now."

"Sammi turned down the Antarctica expedition. She never wanted to leave you. What you heard when Marta was talking to me from the kitchen was just a message I was to give her. If you recall, Sammi had worked out a way to stay in Alaska to be with you and us."

Jake rubbed his eyes as the last two months flashed before his eyes. All of the pain they'd gone through had been pointless.

"I never thought I'd get over the pain of losing my son. Then Sammi came into our lives. It has given me a new reason to get up in the morning. Now she's gone off to the South Pole. I'd hoped you would snap out of this and come talk to me, or go and find her before now. But you're as stubborn as a salmon heading upstream to its death."

Jake stared at Nels. The analogy was true. He *had* been dying. Now, with this new information, he was dying a different kind of death. He'd let the woman of his dreams get away. Over nothing!

"What should I do?"

Nels looked shocked. "Go get her."

"After this, you still want me to be with her?"

"Jake? You've made a big mistake, but you're a good man. You love my Sammi and for some reason she loves you. She's our only tie to Chris. Go bring her home."

That's what he intended to do. "Thank you, Nels."

He got up, grabbed his jacket and headed for the stairs.

"One more thing."

Jake stopped.

"C.J. never meant to hurt you over Lisa. He was eighteen and she was an immature girl who didn't care about anyone's feelings. Sammi isn't Lisa. It's time to let the past go. Your brother loves you and Sammi loves you. Just think about it."

Chapter Eleven

Jake pulled up to the charming cottage Sam had described so many times to him. He felt a spurt of adrenaline, realizing he was about to meet the mother of the woman he loved.

They'd spoken the night before and he knew she would be waiting. Though it was early January in the Napa Valley, it felt like summer to Jake, having come from Alaska. He'd heard there would be mustard flowers in blossom. It was hard to believe such beauty existed in wintertime.

He got out of the rental car and walked to the door, opening the screen door to reach the ceramic tile knocker that said "de Roussillac."

The lovely woman who answered looked too young to be the mother of a twenty-three-year-old. She was taller than Sammi, with green eyes and jaw-length blond hair. Her curvaceous figure was set off by trendy khakis and a green blouson top.

"Hi. You have to be Jake. I'm Andrea de Roussillac. You're right on time." He could feel her eyes examining him. "I would have known you from my daughter's description. Come in."

"Well, hopefully that description was before September."

"Why do you say that?"

"Has Sam called you since then?"

She raised a hand to her throat. "She sent an e-mail, saying she was going to Antarctica on an expedition." A film of moisture glazed Andrea's eyes. "Come in the living room where we can talk."

As he followed her through the French doors, he was struck by a painting of Sam over the fireplace. "That looks just like her. You have a great talent."

"Thank you. Won't you sit down? Can I get you coffee or a soda? I can make you a sandwich."

"I'll have a coffee."

"I'll be back in a minute."

Jake walked around the room, looking at the various pieces of artwork Andrea had created. Sam had told him she painted ceramics, too. She had many talents.

According to Sam, the cottage could be described as shabby-chic, but he could tell this house had been completely remodeled in a contemporary style. In another part of the room was a grouping of photographs Sam must have taken. Four pictures of the vineyard, one in each season.

Soon her mother walked into the room, carrying a tray with their coffee. "Those pictures won Sammi her scholarship to Brooks." She sat down and began to sip while she eyed him. "Obviously there's a reason you phoned me."

"Andrea—I feel inadequate coming to you under these circumstances. I made a horrible mistake that drove Sam away, and it has taken me months to finally track her down."

She sobered. "I made a mistake with her, as well, and wish I had an answer. I don't know if it can be rectified. But that doesn't mean you can't if you find her."

He nodded. "The reason I'm coming to you is that I want to ask you for your daughter's hand in marriage."

"Oh, Jake…"

"I realize you don't know me."

"But I *do* know you, through Sammi. And you're Doug's son, so you have my permission and my blessing. All that's left is for you to find her." Her eyes brimmed with tenderness.

"Thank you, Andrea. Your blessing means everything to me. I want to do this right, and I'm flying to Argentina to get her."

Without words, she got up and hugged him. Jake could feel the worry of a mother who had suffered over Sam just as he had.

"When are you leaving?"

"I finally got a break. A friend of mine in the Coast Guard found out which ship she's on. She'll be arriving tomorrow. I'm flying out to Ushuaia, Argentina, tonight to propose and bring her home."

Andrea hugged him again. "Please—both of you come back safely. Let me walk you out."

JAKE'S HEART RATE WAS off the charts as the *Golden Explorer* pulled into port. He rubbed his eyes, taking in the rugged beauty of Ushuaia, the southernmost city in the world.

It was summer in the Southern Hemisphere, but like Alaska it was chilly, just the way he liked it. A current of air blew off the ocean, bringing with it the aroma of delicious food from nearby shops and restaurants. He could hear exciting musical rhythms coming from the latter.

The longshoremen began to unload the ship's cargo. Each piece coming off seemed to take an eternity. Jake glanced at his watch, counting the minutes. A half hour later the passengers began to disembark.

He could see a couple of good-looking men walking down the gangplank. One stopped to wait for someone. His head turned back and that's when Jake spotted her.

Samantha had only grown more beautiful. As she caught up to the man who'd waited, her long, fair hair fanned out behind her in the breeze. He grabbed her around the shoulders and they walked the rest of the way together, laughing.

Jake felt as if he'd been punched in the stomach. This was not what he'd planned, but it didn't matter. He'd let her go and now had to win her back.

It's now or never, Powell.

Deliberately, he stepped to the middle of the exit so Sam couldn't avoid him. She would have to talk to him no matter what. He watched her go through customs, eager to see her up close.

Nearer to her now, he could hear her joking, but there was no light in her eyes. She appeared to be ten pounds thinner. He wondered if she'd gotten sick on the trip. Or maybe she'd missed him as much as he'd missed her? What a fool he'd been to close the door and walk away from her!

Sam passed through the gate and still didn't notice when she bumped into him. *"Perdón."*

Jake had no intention of moving. "Sam?"

She lifted her head. Her eyes flashed like a lightning bolt and the look of recognition was one he would never forget. "Jake?" As she spoke his name, he knew she was still just as in love with him as he was with her.

"I prefer Smokey."

"What are you doing here? I thought you were one guy who didn't leave America." Her voice shook.

"Well, it's the right climate here, so I thought I'd take a chance."

She laughed. "The right climate?"

"Sam—this is serious," he said. "I should never have let you go. I love you and I…" He got down on one knee and pulled something out of the left pocket of his jacket. "I was going to do this up in the mountains or somewhere romantic, but I can't wait.

"Samantha Danbury, will you marry me?" He opened the box and showed her a brilliant, one-carat, round diamond solitaire set in a platinum band.

Tears spilled from her eyes. "Y-yes," she stammered.

He took the ring out of the box and slid it on her finger. Then he picked her up and crushed her in his arms. Their kiss melted away the pain of the past few months.

A crowd of onlookers began to clap. Some of them were her shipmates, others peddlers in the area. Music began to play and a celebration erupted from nowhere. Jake didn't notice. All he knew was that they were finally together and he had no intention of ever letting Sam go.

"Sam, will you marry me here in Argentina? As Americans we can't marry on Argentinean soil. Do you think the captain of your ship will marry us? I don't want to wait another day to make you my wife."

Samantha looked at the beautiful rugged mountain town and couldn't imagine a more romantic place to wed. She raised her hands to his face, caressing his cheeks. "I'd love to…. Jake?" she whispered in his ear a moment later.

"Yes?"

"I've got to call my mom and tell her."

"I think that's a wonderful idea. I met your mother yesterday and asked her permission for your hand in marriage. Do you have your satellite phone?"

Sam reached in her purse for the sat phone she'd wanted to use a million times at sea. Soon she was dialing her mother's number. Jake heard them greet each other, then she cried, "Mom— I'm getting married!"

THE MAIN HOUSE at the vineyard was bustling with wedding activities. The excitement of getting married again had made Sammi feverish. Her mom had come upstairs to help her dress, and finished zipping up her vintage-style wedding gown.

Sammi was glad she was only three months along in her pregnancy, so she wasn't showing yet. She and Jake had planned on keeping it a secret until today. The simple, white silk dress had braided shoulder straps, with contoured lines showing off her small figure. She had wildflowers from the garden woven among the curls pinned atop her head. The rest of her hair cascaded down to the middle of her back, creating a natural veil "more beautiful than any seamstress could make," Jake had told her.

Sammi wore strappy sandals with heels not too high, since she was scared she might trip walking through the garden. Once she'd finished dressing, she walked over to the bag sitting on the bed and pulled out a small present.

"Happy Mother's Day, Mom."

She watched her mother open it, hoping she would know how much Sammi loved her and that she had forgiven her. The time she'd spent in the Antarctic had brought a new perspective to her life. She realized when it came to matters of the heart, people did things that were unexplainable.

Her mother had made a terrible mistake, but she'd been young and confused. Sammi had tried to put herself in her mom's shoes and imagine losing a husband tragically at age seventeen. As the years went by it must have become more difficult for her to think of a way to tell Sammi the truth. But it didn't matter anymore. That was in the past and it was time to move on.

She saw the delight in her mother's eyes. Sammi had

given her a picture of the two of them taken a couple of years earlier, when they'd gone to Hawaii with her mom's best friend, Nancy, and her family.

While Sammi and Jake had stayed in Argentina for a couple of days, enjoying their honeymoon, they'd combed the shops to find a present to give her mom, and had found a unique frame for the photo.

As Andrea came over and kissed her on the cheek, Sammi gave her a big hug. "I love you, Mom."

"I love you, too, honey. More than you'll ever know."

"Congratulations again on your wedding to Max. I can tell you're happy being married to him. I'm so glad you found love again."

Her mom held Sammi's new baby brother in her arms. Little Max was so adorable it made Sammi excited for the child she and Jake would be having.

"And now it's your wedding day. I'm overjoyed." Andrea put the baby down to reach into her purse, then fastened a bracelet of green gems around her daughter's wrist.

Sammi turned her hand and watched them sparkle, just as she had as a child. "I remember this."

"Chris gave this to me when he found out I was pregnant with you. It's a memento of your father and me."

"Thank you, Mom. I always thought it was special, and now I know why. I'd like to think he's near us today."

"I'm sure he is."

A knock on the door interrupted them. "Sammi? It's time, sweetie," Nels voice called out.

"All right, Grandpa."

Her mother smiled at her. "Are you nervous?"

She smiled back, her eyes blurring. "I'm going to miss you, Mom. Will you, Max and the baby come and visit us often?"

"Of course."

"Good, because I have something special to tell you."

"What is it, darling?"

"I'm pregnant."

"Oh, Sammi." Her mother and little Max hugged her hard. She could see the tears in her mother's eyes. Sammi started to cry, as well.

"Mom, I forgive you and I'm sorry for this year. I know I haven't made it easy. But now that I'm pregnant I'm beginning to understand the reason you lied. My love for this child is so intense already. I love you, Mom."

"Nels? We have a few things for Sammi." Marta's voice echoed in the hall. "Come on, Doris. There isn't much time."

The door opened and in walked two of her favorite women, dressed in spring colors. Doris was in heaven at the vineyard, and had told Doug she had no intention of ever going home. While Marta loved seeing where her granddaughter had grown up, she itched to get back to where she was comfortable.

She called over to Sammi's mom, "Sorry to intrude on your moment, Andrea, but we have a few things we want to give our darling girl."

Sammi watched the whole scene unfold and started giggling. Her mom laughed, too, unable to do anything but acquiesce.

"Me first, Marta. You promised!" Doris exclaimed. "Oh, Samantha—you are a dream. To look like this on your wedding day… Jacob is a fortunate man. Now I just need to find somebody for my Chris." She reached into a bag she was carrying. "I was a Jensen before my wedding, and this is something all Jensen women wear when they marry. It's something borrowed." Doris handed her the sack.

Sammi looked inside, to find a blue, antique lace garter. She could feel herself blushing.

"It's your wedding day, so we have to tease you a little. Now, I want that back. I intend to give it to Chris's wife."

"Okay."

"Put it on, dear. Jacob is waiting!"

Sammi looked to her mom for help. Andrea was all smiles as she helped to lift Sammi's gown and pull off the new one they'd bought, replacing it with the Jensen one.

Marta came over and grasped Sammi's face in her hands. "Samantha, you have no idea the joy you have brought to my life and your grandpa's. The Lord sent us a gift when you came and knocked. Now we have a piece of our son back in our lives."

Sammi's eyes filled with tears. So did Marta's. "We wanted to give you something new, since this is a new beginning for all of us." She reached into her satchel and pulled out a long narrow case. Sammi opened it to discover a choker of pearls. "May I put them on you, dear?"

"Grandma, they're so beautiful! How can I thank you?"

"Oh, don't start that. This is our pleasure. Wear them and know that we love you."

Once they were fastened, Sammi hugged her. "Thank you."

Nels walked in. "Ladies? The wedding. Jake is getting worried."

Sammi turned her head and looked at everyone, touched deeply by the tender moment they'd shared. Then she joined them all in laughter, hearing that Jake was anxious.

"Let's do this, Grandpa."

The other women filed out. Sammi linked her arm in her grandfather's, where it belonged.

"I see you got our gift," he said.

"I love it."

"You are a vision, Samantha Engstrom Powell. Your dad would be so proud of you. *I'm* so proud of you. Thank you for adding his name to yours."

"I wanted his name, Grandpa. And there's one more thing before we go down. I want you to know that Jake and I are three months along with our first baby."

Her grandfather swallowed, then wrapped her in a warm embrace. "You, my dear, have brought a joy to this old man that I never thought would happen again."

"I love you, Grandpa."

"I love you, Samantha. No second thoughts? I could sneak you out the back door if you want."

Her heart palpitated hard as she realized this was really happening.

"Grandpa—you're not supposed to say stuff like that! Especially since I'm already married. Jake told me what you did for us."

"I'm just doing my duty."

They went down the ornate staircase that led to a large vaulted hall with beamed ceilings. The rectangular room was filled with tables covered with flowers from the gardens. Spring had come to the Napa Valley and Sammi had wanted nothing but wildflowers for her wedding.

Since she'd left the vineyard, Max had renovated the entire estate and turned the gardens into a paradise. In the great hall were windows that reached the ceiling, with huge French doors leading out to a deck overlooking the wondrous landscape.

With tables of food and a band in the far corner getting set up for the reception, it was like a dream. Sammi felt she was having an out-of-body experience.

As they approached the stone amphitheater where

everyone was seated, she was so grateful to have her grandpa to hold on to. It was a beautiful place, covered by a wooden trellis, with wisteria in full amethyst bloom. The sun was setting and she could hear the string quartet and harp playing Pachebel's *Canon*.

She would soon see Jake and renew their vows in front in their families. Goose bumps covered her skin. She had loved her first wedding and couldn't understand why she was getting nervous, marrying him again.

Nels guided her down the stone stairway, and the crowd got up from their wooden chairs. But what took her breath away was seeing Jake in a tuxedo, waiting for her under the arbor. He looked so handsome! When their eyes met, any nervous feelings she had about the crowd vanished.

She saw C.J. slap his brother on the back, and wondered what he was saying to him. Jake didn't look away from her, but laughed. She was thrilled to see that her husband had resolved his conflict with his twin and forgiven him. Now they acted like teenagers when they were together.

Dressed in tuxes, the men looked alike if you didn't know them. C.J. was obviously proud to be best man. The brothers were identical in so many ways, but there was a confidence in Jake that made him irresistible.

Then Sammi noticed the handsome blond man standing next to C.J. Her eyes wide, she looked at Jake. He nodded. It was Cole, the doctor who'd seen her act like such a fool.

She was embarrassed all over again, but then started to laugh. She had to fight to remain poised as she walked up the aisle.

Nels came to a stop and passed her hand to Steve. The vintner, her surrogate father, looked so healthy and vibrant. What an amazing change from the man she'd left over a year ago! She bent down and kissed him on the cheek. "I love you, Steve. Thank you for letting us have the wedding here."

"You know how I feel about you," he murmured lovingly.

Max sat next to him and flashed her a tender smile. Sammi gave him a wink and smiled back.

After she straightened, they continued the short walk to the arbor, where her mom and a few of Sammi's friends were waiting. She handed her mother the flowers, then Nels gave her to Jake. Sammi looked at her grandpa. He had tears in his eyes as he kissed her cheek. "Now you take good care of her," he said to Jake.

"I will."

Sammi gazed into Jake's eyes. He couldn't stop staring at her, and a deep contentment enveloped her. "You're so beautiful, Sam," he murmured.

"So are you."

The preacher began the ceremony. As they said their vows for the second time, she knew this was for real.

After hearing the words *You may kiss the bride,* Jake announced loudly, "It's about time."

The whole crowd laughed when he swept Sammi into his arms and whispered in her ear, "This is forever."

* * * * *

*Harlequin Intrigue top author Delores Fossen presents
a brand-new series of breathtaking romantic suspense!*
TEXAS MATERNITY: HOSTAGES
*The first installment available May 2010:
THE BABY'S GUARDIAN*

Shaw cursed and hooked his arm around Sabrina.

Despite the urgency that the deadly gunfire created, he tried to be careful with her, and he took the brunt of the fall when he pulled her to the ground. His shoulder hit hard, but he held on tight to his gun so that it wouldn't be jarred from his hand.

Shaw didn't stop there. He crawled over Sabrina, sheltering her pregnant belly with his body, and he came up ready to return fire.

This was obviously a situation he'd wanted to avoid at all cost. He didn't want his baby in the middle of a fight with these armed fugitives, but when they fired that shot, they'd left him no choice. Now, the trick was to get Sabrina safely out of there.

"Get down," someone on the SWAT team yelled from the roof of the adjacent building.

Shaw did. He dropped lower, covering Sabrina as best he could.

There was another shot, but this one came from a rifleman on the SWAT team. Shaw didn't look up, but he heard the sound of glass being blown apart.

The shots continued, all coming from his men, which meant it might be time to try to get Sabrina to better cover. Shaw glanced at the front of the building.

So that Sabrina's pregnant belly wouldn't be smashed against the ground, Shaw eased off her and moved her to a sitting position so that her back was against the brick wall. They were close. Too close. And face-to-face.

He found himself staring right into those sea-green eyes.

How will Shaw get Sabrina out?
Follow the daring rescue and the heartbreaking
aftermath in THE BABY'S GUARDIAN
by Delores Fossen,
available May 2010 from Harlequin Intrigue.

Copyright © 2010 by Delores Fossen

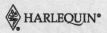

HARLEQUIN®

INTRIGUE®

**BESTSELLING
HARLEQUIN INTRIGUE® AUTHOR**

DELORES FOSSEN

**PRESENTS AN ALL-NEW
THRILLING TRILOGY**

TEXAS MATERNITY: HOSTAGES

When masked gunmen take over the maternity ward
at a San Antonio hospital, local cops, FBI and the scared
mothers can't figure out any possible motive. Before
long, secrets are revealed, and a city that has been on
edge since the siege began learns the truth behind the
negotiations and must deal with the fallout.

LOOK FOR

THE BABY'S GUARDIAN, *May*
DEVASTATING DADDY, *June*
THE MOMMY MYSTERY, *July*

www.eHarlequin.com

HI69472

HARLEQUIN® *Presents*®

Bestselling Harlequin Presents® author

Lynne Graham

introduces

VIRGIN ON HER WEDDING NIGHT

Valente Lorenzatto never forgave Caroline Hales's abandonment of him at the altar. But now he's made millions and claimed his aristocratic Venetian birthright—and he's poised to get his revenge. He'll ruin Caroline's family by buying out their company and throwing them out of their mansion... unless she agrees to give him the wedding night she denied him five years ago....

Available May 2010 from Harlequin Presents!

www.eHarlequin.com

HP12915

is proud to introduce...

New York Times bestselling author

Brenda Jackson

with
SPONTANEOUS

Kim Cannon and Duan Jeffries have a great thing going.
Whenever they meet up, the passion between them
is hot, intense…spontaneous. And things really heat
up when Duan agrees to accompany her to her
mother's wedding. Too bad there's something
he's not telling her.…

Don't miss the fireworks!

*Available in May 2010
wherever Harlequin Blaze books are sold.*

---

red-hot reads

www.eHarlequin.com

HB79542

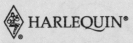

HARLEQUIN®

LAURA MARIE ALTOM

The Baby Twins

Stephanie Olmstead has her hands full raising
her twin baby girls on her own. When she runs
into old friend Brady Flynn, she's shocked to find
herself suddenly attracted to the handsome airline
pilot! Will this flyboy be the perfect daddy—
or will he crash and burn?

"LOVE, HOME & HAPPINESS"

www.eHarlequin.com

HAR75309

Former bad boy Sloan Hawkins is back in
Redemption, Oklahoma, to help keep his aunt's
cherished garden thriving and to reconnect with the
girl he left behind, Annie Markham. But when he
discovers his secret child—and that single mother
Annie never stopped loving him—he's determined
that a wedding will take place in the garden
nurtured by faith and love.

Where healing flows...

Look for

The Wedding Garden

by Linda Goodnight

Available May 2010
wherever you buy books.

Steeple
Hill®

www.SteepleHill.com

LI87595

REQUEST YOUR FREE BOOKS!
2 FREE NOVELS PLUS 2 FREE GIFTS!

HARLEQUIN®

American ★ Romance®

Love, Home & Happiness!

YES! Please send me 2 FREE Harlequin® American Romance® novels and my 2 FREE gifts (gifts are worth about $10). After receiving them, if I don't wish to receive any more books, I can return the shipping statement marked "cancel." If I don't cancel, I will receive 4 brand-new novels every month and be billed just $4.24 per book in the U.S. or $4.99 per book in Canada. That's a saving of at least 15% off the cover price! It's quite a bargain! Shipping and handling is just 50¢ per book.* I understand that accepting the 2 free books and gifts places me under no obligation to buy anything. I can always return a shipment and cancel at any time. Even if I never buy another book from Harlequin, the two free books and gifts are mine to keep forever.

154/354 HDN E5LG

Name _____ (PLEASE PRINT) _____

Address _____ Apt. #

City _____ State/Prov. _____ Zip/Postal Code

Signature (if under 18, a parent or guardian must sign)

Mail to the **Harlequin Reader Service:**
IN U.S.A.: P.O. Box 1867, Buffalo, NY 14240-1867
IN CANADA: P.O. Box 609, Fort Erie, Ontario L2A 5X3

Not valid for current subscribers to Harlequin® American Romance® books.

Want to try two free books from another line?
Call 1-800-873-8635 or visit www.morefreebooks.com.

* Terms and prices subject to change without notice. Prices do not include applicable taxes. N.Y. residents add applicable sales tax. Canadian residents will be charged applicable provincial taxes and GST. Offer not valid in Quebec. This offer is limited to one order per household. All orders subject to approval. Credit or debit balances in a customer's account(s) may be offset by any other outstanding balance owed by or to the customer. Please allow 4 to 6 weeks for delivery. Offer available while quantities last.

Your Privacy: Harlequin is committed to protecting your privacy. Our Privacy Policy is available online at www.eHarlequin.com or upon request from the Reader Service. From time to time we make our lists of customers available to reputable third parties who may have a product or service of interest to you. If you would prefer we not share your name and address, please check here. ☐

Help us get it right—We strive for accurate, respectful and relevant communications. To clarify or modify your communication preferences, visit us at www.ReaderService.com/consumerchoice.

HAR10R

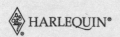
HARLEQUIN®

Showcase

Vicki Lewis Thompson

On sale May 11, 2010

Reader favorites from the most talented voices in romance

Save $1.00 on the purchase of 1 or more Harlequin® Showcase books.

- -

SAVE $1.00 on the purchase of 1 or more Harlequin® Showcase books.

Coupon expires Oct 31, 2010. Redeemable at participating retail outlets.
Limit one coupon per purchase. Valid in the U.S.A. and Canada only.

52609015

Canadian Retailers: Harlequin Enterprises Limited will pay the face value of this coupon plus 10.25¢ if submitted by customer for this product only. Any other use constitutes fraud. Coupon is nonassignable. Void if taxed, prohibited or restricted by law. Consumer must pay any government taxes. Void if copied. Nielsen Clearing House ("NCH") customers submit coupons and proof of sales to Harlequin Enterprises Limited, P.O. Box 3000, Saint John, NB E2L 4L3, Canada. Non-NCH retailer—for reimbursement submit coupons and proof of sales directly to Harlequin Enterprises Limited, Retail Marketing Department, 225 Duncan Mill Rd., Don Mills, ON M3B 3K9, Canada.

U.S. Retailers: Harlequin Enterprises Limited will pay the face value of this coupon plus 8¢ if submitted by customer for this product only. Any other use constitutes fraud. Coupon is nonassignable. Void if taxed, prohibited or restricted by law. Consumer must pay any government taxes. Void if copied. For reimbursement submit coupons and proof of sales directly to Harlequin Enterprises Limited, P.O. Box 880478, El Paso, TX 88588-0478, U.S.A. Cash value 1/100 cents.

5 65373 00076 2   (8100)0 11651

® and TM are trademarks owned and used by the trademark owner and/or its licensee.
© 2009 Harlequin Enterprises Limited

HSCCOUP0410

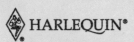
HARLEQUIN®

American ★ Romance®

COMING NEXT MONTH

Available May 11, 2010

#1305 THE BABY TWINS
Babies & Bachelors USA
Laura Marie Altom

#1306 THE MAVERICK
Texas Outlaws
Jan Hudson

#1307 THE ACCIDENTAL SHERIFF
Fatherhood
Cathy McDavid

#1308 DREAM DADDY
Daly Thompson

www.eHarlequin.com

HARCNMBPA0410